IF SHE SAYS YES

TASHA L. HARRISON

DIRTYSCRIBBLER PRESS

ISBN: 978-0-9909403-9-5

❀ Created with Vellum

ALSO BY TASHA L. HARRISON

THE LUST DIARIES

THE TRUTH DUET

A SMALL TOWN ROMANCE: The Malone Sisters

LIQUOR & LAUNDRY

Join my newsletter to get updates on

new releases and free short stories

about your favorite characters!

I'd love to hear from you!

Connect with me at:

Twitter| Instagram | Email

FOLLOW ME ON BOOKBUB!

BECOME A PATRON!

Visit my website:

TashaLHarrison.com

"I am convinced that most people do not grow up ... We marry and dare to have children and call that growing up. I think what we do is mostly grow old. We carry accumulation of years in our bodies, and on our faces, but generally our real selves, the children inside, are innocent and shy as magnolias."

— *MAYA ANGELOU*

1

TOMÁS

Locking myself in an airplane bathroom and beating off like a twelve-year-old as my plane made its descent to Charleston International Airport wasn't something I imagined myself doing at my big age, and yet...

Here I am...

I snarled at my reflection in the tiny bathroom mirror in disgust as I whipped out my already hard dick and dug a bottle of hotel lotion out of my pocket because yes, I'd planned ahead for this moment.

Sage and Summer, the label read.

I found it in the front pocket of my carry-on last night when I was packing and used it to jerk off when I got out of the shower this morning. I wasn't usually the sort of dude that couldn't make it through the day without jerking off, but the situation was dire. Sometimes, taking the edge off was a requirement to function in the world like a human being and not a dick desperate to dive into any wet hole. Well, that wasn't entirely truthful, either. If it was just any wet hole, there'd be no problem. Either way, the cheap hotel lotion had just the right amount of slip to make this jerk-off session quick.

Oh...and one other thing.

I pulled my cell phone out of my pocket and opened my voicemail app. My hand trembled as I selected the most recent message from Darcy MacFarland.

My best friend's mother.

"Hey, Tommy."

She was the only person that still called me Tommy. Hearing my name in her husky, sweet Southern accent? It made my dick throb and was the only reason why I allowed it. But there wasn't much I wouldn't allow Darcy MacFarland to do to me. I popped the lotion open one-handed and squeezed a generous dollop of the slippery cream into my palm.

"Seems like we're playing phone tag, but I wanted to let you know that I received your email with the very detailed itinerary. I've synced my calendar with yours to make sure there are no issues with keeping our boy on schedule. However... I did see that you have reservations at The Mills House Hotel. Well, I have to say that I don't approve. I thought both of my boys were going to stay here with me!"

My boys. Fisting my dick in my hand, I gave it a slippery tug. That shouldn't be hot, but in my twisted brain, any sort of possession from Darcy triggered this kind of response.

"I have the garçonnière all set up for you. You've stayed there before, but I've had it remodeled since then, so hopefully, it will be up to the standards of the wunderkind architect of one of the fastest-growing firms in Chicago."

She let out a deep, husky chuckle, and just the intimate sound of her laughter brought me close to the edge.

"That will always tickle me. My little Tommy on the cover of *Architectural Digest.* Hm. I guess both of you boys are all grown up now. Anyway, I hope you'll go ahead and cancel those reservations after you hear this message. If you stayed in a hotel, it would make me very upset. And you don't want to upset me, do you?"

No...never. I only want to please you.

"Any ol' way, I look forward to seeing you tomorrow. It's been so long. Until then, sweetie!"

I've missed you too. More than you could ever know.

I closed my eyes and imagined how she would respond if I told her how much I missed her — how much I fantasized about her and how dirty those fantasies were. Would she console me when I confessed my years-long crush? No...she'd probably laugh at me. Maybe she wouldn't believe me until I explained in detail how much I wanted to bury my face between her legs. Or maybe she would shame me a little (or a lot) for being so obsessed with her. But then...maybe...she would make me beg. God, I wanted to beg for her. Beg for her kisses. For her touch. For her taste.

"Fuck..." My whimpering sounded so loud in the tiny bathroom, but it was hard to keep those sounds in when I thought about Darcy letting me worship her pussy or using my body to get herself off. My dick throbbed in my hand as I fucked my fist a little faster, imagining that I was doing it for Darcy — coming for Darcy.

The first spurt hit the wall just over the faucet, but I was too inside of my own head — inside of this fantasy — to be appropriately horrified by it as I fucked the sensitive tip of my dick into my slippery hand, milking every last drop of pleasure out of my orgasm.

Light-headed and panting, I leaned over the sink and pressed my forehead against the tiny mirror. My breath fogged and obscured my reflection, and honestly, I was glad because the shame that always accompanied this fantasy was quick on the heels of my euphoric release.

Swallowing down my disgust, I reached blindly for a few paper towels and turned on the faucet to clean myself up.

This is ridiculous.

After all these years, I still had an unbearable crush on my best friend's mom, and it didn't look like it was going to end any time soon. I wasn't entirely sure what I was supposed to do about it. And considering the way that I wanted her, I knew this was something I could never confess — to her or anyone.

I realized a few years ago that I was what people in the lifestyle called a submissive. Not in the way that I wanted a woman clad in shiny latex to crush my balls with her spiked heels — even though I have tried that. Hey, a guy couldn't really know what he liked if he didn't try everything, right? But my fantasies about Darcy were...very *Darcy*-specific. I wanted to worship her. Cater to her in ways I assumed other men never have. What was that even called? A slave? A pet?

Fuck. My dick liked both of those labels.

It had been about seven years since I last saw Darcy, though I'd thought about her nearly every day of those seven years. Her son, Jared, has been my best friend since college. I was the broke out-of-state student, piecing my tuition together with scholarships, grants, and part-time jobs, who couldn't afford the trip home to Chicago every holiday. Jared was the one with a rich family and a fun-loving mom who threw pool parties that nearly got her ousted from their historic downtown Charleston neighborhood. She was also the one who came to my rescue my junior year when my grades plummeted due to too much partying, and I lost one of my scholarships. She let me stay in the garçonnière rent-free. Let me borrow her old car — a late-model Mercedes — to get back and forth to campus. Fed me from her table most nights. I think I fell in love with her that summer. Well, to be honest, I was halfway in love with her before that or at least deeply infatuated.

Jesus... The way my heart used to pound in my chest every time I heard her ask Jared, "Are you coming home this weekend? If you are, bring Lil' Tommy with you!" And I accepted every invitation eagerly.

Lil' Tommy.

I outgrew that nickname long before I went to college, demanded that everyone call me Tomás, but for Darcy? I would be her Lil' Tommy any time, any place.

Which would be so much easier to do if she wasn't my best friend's mother.

My friendship with Jared was important to me. After graduation, we both moved to Chicago, my hometown. He went to medical school at the University of Illinois and then became a doctor at Northwestern. I started an entry-level job at Edgewater Associates, one of the most elite architecture firms in the city. That job gave me the foundation to start my own firm, Son of Martin, five years ago. Jared was my biggest supporter, then and now, so, of course, I said yes when he asked me to be his best man. I mean, what the fuck was I supposed to say? *Sorry, bro. I can't be your best man because just hearing your mother call me Lil' Tommy makes me weak with the need to be inside of her?* No, of course not. I couldn't tell my best friend of fifteen years that I've been fantasizing about his mother as long as we've known each other. Besides, I was honored that he asked me to stand at his side while he recited his vows to Brandi. I just hoped I could make it through the ceremony without coming in my pants.

Four days. Four days and three nights in the guesthouse, mere steps from her bed.

I cursed again, finally meeting my reflection in the mirror. Took in my flushed face and rumpled clothing. I barely recognized myself. I buttoned my pants and smoothed down the front of my t-shirt, attempting to put myself back to rights.

How the fuck am I going to survive the next four days?

To be honest, I wasn't sure I would, and if I did, my dick would probably be really chafed from fucking my own hand.

———

WE MADE our way toward baggage claim once we touched down. The car service I'd hired pinged me while we waited for our luggage at the carousel, and I felt that satisfying dopamine hit I always got when my plans came together seamlessly. Beside me, Jared groaned audibly.

"Can you not have your face buried in your phone this weekend?" he complained.

"I was just confirming our ride," I said, stuffing my phone back into my pocket. "You do realize that I'll have to look at my phone to make sure everything stays on schedule, right?"

"I get that, but I swear to god if I catch you responding to work emails—"

"I'm not. I've got my office manager on everything until I get back. There's nothing important enough to distract me from getting the most out of this weekend," I reassured him.

And that was partially true. I'd landed one of the biggest and most prestigious contracts of my career before we left Chicago. Signed the paperwork on it right before I got on the plane. But as the owner of my own fledgling architecture firm, it was difficult to pull back entirely. I was gonna give it my best effort for my best friend.

I spotted my and Jared's bags on the turnstile and grabbed them both. "Car's waiting out front."

The driver took us the long way around from the airport, which was fine because it was a great reintroduction to the city I came of age in. He turned on Meeting Street and drove right through the thick of it, past Marion Square, all the way down to South Battery. Charleston and its small-town charm rolled out before us. I fell in love with the city and its historic architecture all over again.

The reason why — well, one of the reasons why — I'd wanted to attend the College of Charleston was that the B.A. program had a focus on historic preservation and community planning — which was the exact mission of my firm, Son of Martin. The other reason was that it was far from Chicago and so different from the steel and concrete urban environment that I grew up in that it forced me to open my mind to new experiences.

College of Charleston was on the coast of South Carolina in Summerville. The air was hot and heavy with water, time moved slower, and even the most stressful parts of my course of study seemed like languid, dreamy days when I looked back on them now.

Driving to the MacFarland family home filled me with nostalgia as well. The palmetto trees, magnolias heavy with fragrant white blossoms, and colorful flowers that poured from the window boxes of narrow townhomes on cobblestone streets were quaint and quintessentially Southern. I rolled the window down and breathed in the mix of floral and brackish-scented air coming off the Ashley River. I could already feel that second hand slowing. This was my first vacation from my high-stress life in over a year. I was well overdue.

The wedding was on Saturday evening, but we'd flown in early because Darcy had stressed that it was important to her to spend some time with her son before the nuptials. Jared was also worried that Brandi and his mother hadn't bonded enough...whatever that meant. But I was glad to have a little extra time on our schedule so all of the pre-wedding preparations wouldn't feel rushed.

"Fuck," Jared groaned while thumbing out a text.

"What's up?"

"I asked my Aunt Amelia to find mom a date to the wedding and she just told me that mom refused to even consider it."

"A date? I thought she was seeing that realtor guy—"

"Todd?" Jared spat his name out like it tasted foul. "Nah, that was just a fling. She hasn't dated anyone since Dad died."

"No fucking way..." I said, realizing belatedly that I was way too shocked and possibly visibly delighted at this news. Darcy was single... I mean, she was still my best friend's mother, but if I flirted a little bit, I didn't have to worry about stepping on another man's toes.

"Yeah, well, none of this would be an issue if Jojo and Dylan weren't coming."

Jolene Kirkland. Shannon MacFarland's long time mistress and mother of his now ten year old son.

District Attorney Shannon MacFarland's wandering eye was never a secret — especially not to me and Jared. We'd parted ways many a night on King Street, leaving his dad with some girl half his age. I was ashamed to say I didn't think twice about it back then. At twenty-one, the concept of marriage was foreign to me. I just assumed cheating was part of it. All men cheated on their wives, right? I mean, both of our fathers had cheated, so that proved to be true for me and Jared. But it was still a shock when Jojo showed up at his funeral with a three-year-old kid. And Darcy... I could hardly believe how gracious she was to Jojo and her son — then and now.

"Anyway, I know you're here to be my best man, but Mom's been in a funk. She's always liked you. Maybe you can keep her happy and distracted this weekend, so they don't kill each other?"

Oh fuck...he doesn't even realize what he's asking me to do. Keep Darcy happy and distracted? Seriously? "Of course, Jay. Assuming she even needs it. I'm sure she'll be busy with wedding preparations since y'all are having it at the house. And she probably found a date on her own." Though the thought of that made me want to clench my fists.

"I doubt it," Jared said, shaking his head. "She hasn't mentioned that she's dating anyone, so she's probably attending alone."

It was shocking that a woman as fine as Darcy MacFarland wasn't dating anyone? How? Why? If I had half a chance, I would be beating down her door...with my fucking dick. "That's just criminal," I muttered under my breath.

"I know. Mom deserves to be happy, you know? At least for this weekend. So, you'll take care of her for me? Make sure her wine glass is full and dance with her or whatever? Turn on that Tomás Martinez charm?" He elbowed me playfully.

Dance...? Darcy loved to dance and was a phenomenal dancer. I'd seen her in action. I never danced with her because her husband was always around. I guess I would get my chance this weekend. I was no slouch, but I didn't think she would let me push her around the dance floor. But the thought of Darcy's body pressed against mine while dancing a slow bachata or a banda with my thigh wedged up against her pussy...

"Yeah, sure. I can do all that." I squirmed in my seat. *I might die, but I can do it.*

"Thanks, man. I just want to make sure she's okay and has a good time this weekend."

The driver took us down Rainbow Row, one of the most photographed streets in the Holy City, and turned into what appeared to be an alley, albeit a cleaner, wider alley than I had ever found in Chicago. The driver pulled into a space next to a big, black Range Rover. The garage was open, and inside I could see an AMG Benz, low-slung and bright red. That had to be Darcy's. Alongside the garage was a brick pathway that led to the back entrance of the MacFarland townhome. All the nervous energy that I'd barely kept at bay bubbled up inside of me as we grabbed our suitcases out of the trunk and made our way toward the house. Zinnias crowded the walkway. The strong floral scent was overwhelming, and I felt like that twenty-two-year-old kid, dying for his crush to throw a smile his way.

Just beyond the red brick entryway, the residence buzzed with activity. The courtyard and porches were getting decorated with white and pink peonies. In the yard was a huge archway of the same flowers on a raised platform that would be the altar.

"Holy shit," Jared cursed in a soft voice as he stood on the porch, looking out over the yard.

"What?" I asked, concerned that something was amiss.

"I'm really getting married."

I laughed and clapped my friend on the shoulder. "Yep, it's really happening. You're not getting cold feet, are you?"

Jared shook his head and smiled. "Absolutely not. Brandi is it for me, but seeing all these decorations and shit does make me feel nervous."

Through the kitchen, another door led to another narrow brick walkway that opened onto a wide side garden. Just ahead was a sparkling pool where someone was swimming laps.

"Mr. MacFarland, and Mr. Martinez," a clipped Southern voice greeted, and we both looked up to see the MacFarland family butler — a stern woman named Minerva Griffiths.

"Minerva! You're still alive! I had no idea," Jared joked.

And even though I knew that they had always shared this antagonistic humor, it still made me cringe. I felt uncomfortable in the presence of obvious wealth, even though I had some of my own now.

"Still insufferable, I see," Minerva said drolly.

"Come now, Minnie! You haven't seen me since Thanksgiving. Give us a kiss!"

Minerva swatted at him. "Don't you dare put your lips on me, you bratty toddler! I can't believe you convinced that nice girl to marry you. She'll live to regret it. You mark my words."

Jared smacked a kiss on her cheek anyway, and Minerva blushed bright red. "Where's my mother?"

The lady butler rolled her eyes. "Swimming. She's always in the pool nowadays."

My friend shrugged. "There's worse things."

"Will you be staying in your old bedroom?"

"Yes, I will be, but I think mother said she set Tomás up in the garçonnière—"

"Jesus," I scoffed.

"What?"

"Garçonnière? Minerva's right. You are a spoiled brat."

"I always did like you," Minerva said with a smile. "Leave your bags here, and I'll make sure they get to your rooms and unpacked."

"Oh, if you don't mind, Minerva, I'd like to unpack my own bag."

"Why can't Minnie unpack your bag? What are you hiding in there? Your pocket pussy?"

I elbowed him hard. "The fuck, man?"

"I'm just saying, it's been a while since you've talked about a woman in any significant way. If you did have a pocket pussy in your carry-on, I wouldn't judge."

"I'd hate to mar your pretty face three days before your wedding," I growled through clenched teeth. It was an empty threat. I loved this man like a brother, but he was really embarrassing the shit out of me right now.

"Relax," Jared said, giving me a lazy smile. "I know you're too uptight for that. Come on. Let's go say hey to mom."

I followed Jared into the house, then through the French doors to the balustrade that ran the length of the townhome — down here, they called them piazzas. The junior Olympic-size pool was just beyond the porch, and I could see Darcy slicing her way through the water.

"Hey, mom!" Jared called out.

Darcy stopped mid-stroke and treaded water while she squinted in our direction. "Jared? Tommy? Hey!" she exclaimed before she dove under the surface and swam to the edge of the pool.

"Oh, shit," I said breathlessly as she climbed out of the water.

I shouldn't stare, especially since I was standing next to her son — my best friend — but fuck...

Darcy was wearing an orange swimsuit with cut-outs that revealed her flat belly and toned back. The color contrasted and complimented her smooth golden saddle-brown skin. She turned to grab her towel, and water trailed off her two braids and down her back, drawing my attention to her ass. The ass-to-waist ratio made the rise of her hips the perfect place for me to hold her if I—

Not now, damn it.

But goddamn, this woman was still as beautiful as I remembered. Her angular teardrop face didn't sport a single wrinkle until she smiled — full lips parting and her wide light brown eyes twinkling as she regarded us both. She pulled on a caftan, hiding all of that gorgeous skin. The loose fabric did nothing to hide the slow roll of her hips as she made her way toward us, though. A bright smile graced her lips as she climbed the steps.

"My gorgeous son," she said, cupping Jared's cheek like he was a kid and not a thirty-four-year-old man about to get married.

"Hey, mommy," Jared crooned and kissed his mother.

She turned toward me, and I swear my heart punched out of my chest like a cartoon wolf with hearts for eyes.

"Hey, Ms. MacFarland," I stammered.

Darcy rolled her eyes and swatted my shoulder. "How many times do I have to tell you to call me Darcy?"

My cheeks heated a little from her light scolding. "It just seems disrespectful."

"Nonsense," she said with a sweet smile on her face. "I'm Darcy to you." She moved in close and cupped my cheeks in her hands. "Sweet lil' Tommy... It's been too long. I'd hug you, but I'm all wet!"

And then she kissed me — on the cheek, but it was still a kiss — and I felt like I might faint because all of the blood in my body had suddenly rushed to my dick.

"I'm so glad you boys came out here early. Are you hungry?" she asked, turning to Jared, still holding my face in her hands.

"Starved," Jared groaned.

"Okay, let me go up and get dressed, and we'll go to that place you like." She turned her attention back to me and looked me right in the eye. "Lil' Tommy Martinez," she said again in a soft voice that felt like it was just for me.

I'm not little where it matters. I bit my bottom lip to hold in that declaration, and her eyes tracked the movement. Not for the first time, I wondered if she did that to create some distance between us. As if calling me Lil' Tommy helped her see me as a kid and not the grown ass man who's always had eyes for her. Either way, the nickname has never made me feel infantilized or disrespected. It felt as intimate as her hands holding my face.

"Mom...his name is Tomás. No one calls him Tommy anymore," Jared said.

"She can call me Tommy if she wants," I said. My voice was way too low and way too suggestive and probably gave too much away.

"Seriously? I know how much you hate it," my friend asked just as his cell phone began to ring. "It's Brandi. Let me talk to her right quick." Jared walked a few paces away, but I barely registered it because Darcy was still touching me, looking right into my eyes.

"So, which is it, Tommy or Tomás?" she asked, emphasizing *más* as if she wanted more. And fuck if I didn't want to give it to her.

"I meant what I said. You can call me whatever you want," I said again, trying and nearly failing to keep my mouth and my body a respectable distance from hers.

The corners of her bright eyes squinted just the tiniest bit, and a smile quirked one corner of her mouth. "Well, I like Tommy. You've always been my Lil' Tommy," she said, giving my cheek an affectionate pat and then letting me go.

Yes, ma'am, I have.

2

TOMÁS

While Darcy dressed, I hoped I would be able to run to the garçonnière — such a fucking pretentious word — to unpack and jerk off again, but Jared followed me up the steps to the small two-bedroom apartment over the garage. He was still talking to Brandi, but now she was on speaker, asking about the bachelor party.

"I really hope that he hasn't planned some last hurrah fuck session with one of your grimy ex-girlfriends," she said with a little more attitude than I was accustomed to hearing from her.

I turned to Jared and gave him a questioning look, and he just rolled his eyes and shrugged his shoulders.

"Babe, I don't know what Tomás has planned, but I'm sure he's not lining up some sort of last-minute fuck session with any of my grimy ex-girlfriends. Right, best man?" He thrust the phone under my chin.

"Uh..." I stammered, caught off-guard. "No grimy exes. I promise."

"That sounds like a lie, Tomás. I've never known you to be a liar."

The laugh that bubbled out of me at that statement was

genuine because, of course, I'm a liar. No, I wasn't lying about keeping Jared away from his grimy exes — who had most certainly started circling the moment they learned of his engagement. But I was lying to myself and everyone about being this strait-laced dude who didn't even want to be accused of packing a pocket pussy. I was lying when I pretended to receive that affection from Darcy as purely maternal when my dick was hard as fuck. She fucking touched me and kissed me. I would most certainly let her do—

"Bro!" Jared stage-whispered, pulling me back into the present.

Right. I was supposed to convince his fiancée that there would be no exes on the agenda tomorrow night. I took the phone and paced away from Jared. "Brandi, hasn't Jay always been faithful to you?"

"I mean, yes, but—"

"So why would he stop now?"

"I don't know, but—"

"And have you seen pictures of his exes?" I asked, in full negotiation mode now.

She chuckled. "Yeah, I have."

"Brandi, you're the prettiest girl he's ever dated, and you put up with his childish, spoiled ass even better than I do, and I've known him for years."

"I suspect that's because I can suck his dick to get him to do anything that I want, but you're right."

"Whoa-ho-ho! Ma'am!" Jared exclaimed, snatching the phone out of my hand and taking it off speaker. "Why are you airing our business out like that?"

Laughing, I grabbed my carry-on and my suitcase and rolled it into the nearest bedroom. Darcy wasn't kidding when she had the apartment remodeled. When I stayed here, it was wall-to-wall carpet, cheap tile in the kitchenette and bathroom, and a fiberglass tub and shower insert. Now, hardwood floors graced the common areas. The bedrooms were carpeted with a higher-end product, and the big Jack and Jill bathroom that connected the bedrooms was now tiled from floor to ceiling with grey subway tile and had a big glass shower enclosure. It was nice when I lived here, but now it would be easy to rent out if she ever needed to do that. That made me wonder if she'd remodeled it with that purpose in mind. She was a widow. Was money an issue now?

That is none of your business, Tomás.

But it was hard not to worry about her now. Darcy was a broker with her own agency, so I was sure she wasn't destitute now that Shannon was gone. But there was Jolene to worry about. I'd heard horror stories about spiteful mistresses tying up their lover's estate in probate court. Was Jolene the spiteful sort? Had Shannon convinced her that Darcy was some horrible, cold fish of a wife who deserved to be cheated on? From what I could remember, he certainly had no problem talking about his wife as if she were a burden and not the love of his life.

Damn.

It was strange that I remembered all of that now and saw it from a different perspective. It made my heart ache for Darcy. Who was taking care of her and her needs now?

I want to be the one taking care of her needs. All of them.

I palmed my dick and eyed the door to the Jack and Jill bathroom. Had I spent too much time contemplating Darcy's mental and emotional well-being, or did I still have time to take the edge off (again)?

Standing in the open doorway, I listened to see if Jared was still in the apartment. Damn it, he was, but he was still on the phone with Brandi, so maybe I had enough time to handle my business.

As quietly as I could, I backed up into the room with my

thumb on the button of my shorts. But before I could get the door closed, Jared was on the other side, pushing his way in.

"Mom just sent me a text to say she was ready to go. Are you about done in here?" he asked.

"Uh... yeah," I said hesitantly. "Lemme just use the bathroom right quick."

"Cool, no problem," he said, then flopped onto the bed.

I clenched my teeth. This was my best friend who lacked boundaries and constantly barreled through mine. There was no fucking way I was going to get him out of this room long enough for me to rub one out.

"I'll just be a second," I said, then ducked into the bathroom and closed the door.

"Hey, by the way, sorry if mom was like...inappropriate or whatever. I think she forgets that we aren't kids sometimes, you know? It's just in her nature to baby us."

Was that what she was doing down by the pool? Why did my dick say differently?

"I think it's sweet, but Brandi thinks it's weird, so I know it can be a little off-putting sometimes," Jared continued.

I rolled my eyes and unzipped my flies. "Why are you talking to me about your mom like I didn't live with her for most of my junior and senior year of college?" I asked, reaching into my underwear to adjust my dick so that it wasn't tenting the front of my shorts in an obscene way. "It's no big deal, Jay. I know your mom can be...affectionate and nurturing."

"Yeah, I'm just saying. That shit might be on ten now. You haven't been around since the funeral."

I frowned. This was the second time my usually unobservant friend had said something about how Darcy was reacting to his father's death. Was he more concerned about his mother than he was letting on?

And here I was daydreaming about bending his mother over

this quartz bathroom counter. That deflated my dick faster than anything had in the last month or so of planning this wedding with Darcy. I zipped up my shorts, washed my hands, and opened the door to the bedroom. "You're really worried about her, aren't you?" I asked.

"Yeah, kinda," he said without looking me in the eyes. "She just hasn't been herself, you know? If I knew that letting Dylan be the ring bearer at my wedding was going to cause this much drama, I wouldn't have included him. But he's my little brother. It's not our fault we had such a shitty dad."

"I get it." Unlike me, Jared was an only child. He was one hundred percent into forming a relationship the moment he knew about Dylan's existence. But, again, that had to be hard for Darcy to stomach. "Don't worry. I'll keep Darcy happy and distracted this weekend. I've got my marching orders."

Jared grimaced. "It's weird as fuck to hear you call my mother by her first name," he said as he climbed off the bed. "Even more weird, that you're letting her call you Tommy. I thought you hated that shit."

"I do...except when Darcy does it," I said with a waggle of my eyebrows.

"Yeah, no. I don't even like the implication of that look. Don't turn the Martinez charm on full blast," he warned. "And don't think I didn't hear you curse under your breath when she got out of the pool. Keep her happy, but keep it PG, *Tommy*. I know how you like the older ladies."

"Jared MacFarland, what exactly are you accusing me of? I'm a gentleman," I said, covering my heart with my hand.

Jared narrowed his eyes at me. "You're right," he said finally. "But, I hope you're not too much of a gentleman to give me a debauched bachelor party."

"Debauched? That's a big word for you."

"And I hope my weekend lives up to it."

I clapped him on the shoulder. "Don't worry. I've got it covered."

————

CHARLESTON HAS ALWAYS BEEN the sort of city that you eat your way through. In the years since I'd spent any real time here, that had become even more true. Quite a few new restaurants had been added to the roster, and Jared's favorite spot, a place called The Butcher & The Bee, was one of them.

"Good afternoon, y'all! Do you have a reservation?" the hostess asked cheerfully.

"Uh, no. Can we sit outside, though? You boys don't mind, do you?"

"Mom, it's like ninety degrees outside," Jared complained.

"But I'm in a sundress. I'll freeze to death in this air conditioning," Darcy complained, rubbing her bare arms.

"We've got some fans out there. I can make sure y'all are seated near one," the hostess suggested.

"Perfect compromise," I said, pulling the door open again.

"Thank you, Tommy," Darcy purred as she gathered the hem of her long, gauzy sundress and followed the hostess to our table.

Darcy was chic and bohemian in her long, striped linen sundress, with flat braided sandals on her narrow feet, and her hair pulled up into a messy and still slightly wet bun. She looked fit, sun-kissed, and half her age, but totally different in some distinct way from the woman I knew years ago. More relaxed, maybe? More comfortable in her skin?

"You know...you probably wouldn't be so cold all the time if you had some meat on your bones," Jared teased as he pulled out her chair.

"Meat on my bones?" she countered with a raised brow, her eyes hidden behind dark sunglasses.

"Yeah," he said, grabbing the other chair that was completely shaded, which left me with my back in the scorching sun. "All that swimming has made you too lean."

"Whatever," Darcy said with a dismissive wave. "I'm in the best shape of my life."

"I know that's right," the hostess cosigned while passing out the menus. "You look damn good for a woman who has a son his age."

"She looks damn good, period," I corrected before I was able to censor the thought. I didn't have a chance to regret it, though, because the compliment brought the prettiest smile to Darcy's lips.

"Thank you, Tommy," she said. "I wish my son could just give his mother a compliment without the critique." She raised an eyebrow at him again.

"Come on, mom. You know you're beautiful, but men in your age bracket tend to like their women a lil' bit thicker."

Darcy scoffed. "First of all, I lost the weight for me. Not to attract a man. I'll have you know that I have no interest in dating right now. I'm just trying to do me. And secondly, if I were interested in dating, what makes you think I'd be looking for a man my age?"

Oh, shit!

"Mom! Are you saying that you're a cougar?"

Please, say yes. Please, say yes, and I'll be your cub.

"Oh, Jared, calm down. I just said that I'm not dating and have no plans to date. I may, however, take a younger lover if I feel the need."

Jesus Christ. Was she for real or just joking around to wind Jared up? Her eyes were still hidden behind her dark sunglasses, so I couldn't tell. But even if she was, the mere implication that she might be interested in taking a younger man as her lover had my fucking heart doing a jig in my chest.

"Seriously, ma? That is completely inappropriate."

"Men do it all the time. Why can't I? What about you, Tommy? Do you think it's inappropriate?" She looked at me with a smirk on her face that said she knew exactly what I thought of her dating younger men, and that inappropriate wasn't a label I would stick on it.

"Jared... I think that you need to consider the fact that Darcy is a damn fine woman and would have her choice of men — young or not — if she decided to start dating," I said diplomatically.

"That's not what I meant, and you know it," Jared countered.

"Okay, boys. Let it drop. I'm not dating anyone, Jared. You have nothing to worry about. However..." She turned her attention to me again. "Since we're on the subject of relationships, can you explain why you're attending this wedding without a plus-one, Tommy? I assumed you would show up with some fine young thing on your arm."

"Well, I'm—"

"Tomás doesn't date," Jared interrupted. "He's practically a fucking monk."

"—not dating anyone," I finished, cringing at the way he just blurted out the details of my personal life. "I just don't have the time right now. I'm focused on my business."

"Gorgeous, successful guy like you? Seems like you wouldn't have to make time because you can have whomever you choose, whenever you choose."

It was hard not to preen when she called me gorgeous, but somehow, I managed not to puff out my chest.

"And he does. This man once had a woman break into his apartment, tie herself to the bed, and wait for him."

"She didn't break in," I corrected. "The doorman let her in—"

"Either way, she was naked in your bed, and you just sent her home."

I shrugged. "I wasn't interested."

"A woman got naked and tied herself to your bed, and you weren't interested?" Darcy asked.

"He's not telling the whole story—"

"You're right. Maybe she needs a visual," Jared said, pulling his phone out. He did what I presumed was a quick internet search then handed the phone to Darcy.

"Uh...wow," she said, both eyebrows arrowing upward. "Chicago's sexy weather girl was naked in your bed, and you sent her home?"

"Not exactly? There's more to the story."

Marlowe Thompson and I had met at one of those black-tie events where you bought a plate of rubbery chicken and mushy salad for fifteen hundred dollars just to be in the room where it happens. I was wearing a rented tux and had bought my seat at the table with new money. I was young and brown, and I felt inconspicuous in that room. Marlowe, an outgoing and well-connected woman, spotted me and attached herself to my side. She was gorgeous with dark skin the color of warm roasted walnuts and brown eyes that caught and held the sunlight. She should have been it for me.

"That woman stalked you for months, and you never pulled the trigger — not even when she conned her way into your bed."

"Well, that's not exactly true." If we were gonna get specific, she'd tied herself to my bed after I'd expressed my need for submission — completely misinterpreting it. After that, I decided that if she couldn't pay close enough attention when I revealed my most intimate thoughts and feelings with her, it was a waste of time. "We did...connect a couple of times, but it really just boiled down to the fact that we were two busy people who couldn't make it work. Like I said..."

"You were busy and uninterested," Darcy finished for me, her eyes narrowed suspiciously. "Sounds like you're using work as an excuse."

I shrugged. "You've seen my calendar. If you scroll back through the last twelve months, you'll see that this is my first vacation in over a year."

She frowned and pulled her phone out of her Gucci bag. A couple of taps and swipes of her thumb resulted in a series of tsks and head shaking. "I can't say that I approve of this, Tommy. I think I'll give you strict instructions to have fun this weekend."

"That's the plan," I said with a nod.

"Speaking of which, you all need to be at the hotel to meet the groomsmen in an hour, and I'm supposed to go for a final fitting at the seamstress. We better go ahead and order."

I nodded and opened the menu. "What do you usually get, Jay?"

"I usually get the ribs, but that seems a little heavy if we're going to a steakhouse later. I think I'm gonna get the veggie burger instead."

"Hmm. That sounds good, but..." I eyed the menu, but nothing jumped out at me.

"How hungry are you, Tommy? If you're not too ravenous, we can just get a bunch of shareable plates to split between the two of us."

I shrugged. "Sure, but I still—"

"I'll order for us," she said with such decisive finality that it made my dick twitch.

What the fuck was it about that hint of the bossiness that made me want to feed her everything she'd just ordered to her with my fingers?

Darcy ordered things that I probably wouldn't have chosen for myself — bacon-wrapped dates, whipped feta with fermented honey and black pepper served with triangles of pita bread, a crispy avocado salad topped with shrimp, a celery root pancake, and mixed spring greens. She insisted that I take my share first, but I ended up preparing her plate, which gave me a weird sense of pleasure that had me daydreaming about serving her in other ways.

Once our plates were clean, I ducked inside as the busboy cleared the table to pay the tab. Darcy was already footing so much of the bill for Jared's wedding. I didn't want her to feel obligated to cover this one.

When I got back to the table, they were already gathering their things.

"Listen here, young man," Darcy said, hoisting her big designer bag on one shoulder while hooking her hand into the bend of my elbow. "I don't like this sneaky business of you paying the bill. I'm a wealthy woman—"

"I know. And I'm a wealthy man. How would it look to let you pay for my meal?"

"Like someone who allows a woman who cares for him to take care of him."

That made an involuntary smile come to my lips. "I think in this scenario, you're the one who needs to be taken care of."

Darcy's steps slowed, and she lifted her sunglasses. I did the same so that I could look into her eyes. "This is how you do it, huh?" she asked, a bemused smile on her lips and a slightly wary look in her eyes.

"Do what?"

"Make a girl so desperate for your attention that she breaks into your apartment, strips naked, and ties herself to your bed," she clarified with a smirk.

"Hm, it might be a little hint of it. Why do you ask? Should I expect you to be waiting in my bed wearing nothing but your gorgeous golden skin?"

Darcy's light brown eyes stared into mine for a long moment as if she was trying to assess my seriousness. In that moment, they took a noticeable trip down to my lips and across the breadth of my shoulders.

"I can see how it works," she said, sliding her sunglasses back in place with a smirk.

"I mean, I can turn on the charm if you want a real demonstration."

"I think that taste was enough for this old lady."

"First of all, you're not old, and secondly, that wasn't nearly enough. A woman like you deserves to be charmed and wooed and wor—"

"Slight change of plans," Jared interrupted as he picked up a light jog to catch up to us. "I need to meet Brandi at the jeweler so we can pick up our wedding bands—"

"But that's on the schedule for tomorrow—"

"That's why it's a slight change of plans, cruise director. Ma, can you drop Tomás off at the hotel?"

"I can just catch an Uber—"

"Absolutely not. I'll drop you off at hotel. I have to head that way to do some last-minute errands anyway. Besides, it'll give us a chance to finish this conversation," she said, giving my bicep a gentle squeeze. I barely resisted the urge to flex under that hand, but I did register a hum of appreciation as her fingers molded over the muscle.

"A'ight. Brandi is gonna swing by here to get me. I'll catch up with y'all later. Just text me to let me know where you guys land."

I stifled the urge to sigh. "You have a calendar. That's the whole purpose of—"

"Got it. Right." He yanked me into a hug and pounded me

on the back, kissed his mother on the cheek, then trotted around the building to where I presumed Brandi would pick him up.

In the car, Darcy took a moment to put some sunblock on her face and shoulders before opening the Benz's moonroof. I didn't bother trying not to stare now. There had always been this sort of easy flirting between Darcy and me, and now that we'd reestablished that dynamic, I didn't see the need to hide my interest. She caught me looking and smiled.

I'd set the groomsmen up at the Mills House Hotel. It was on Meeting Street in the heart of historic Charleston and had the sort of tropical charm that I wanted to revisit while I was in town. Staying at Darcy's was infinitely better, of course. Anywhere that put me in close proximity of the long brown legs she flashed while getting comfortable behind the steering wheel was a place I wanted to be.

"So, how is Jared doing with all of this? Any cold feet or second-guessing on his part?"

I laughed. "Not even a little bit. I think he's finally met his match with Brandi."

A little smile quirked her lips. "I believe you're right. She's a nice enough girl. A little pushy, but she means well."

Brandi was a born and bred Chicagoan, which was a personality in complete contrast with Jared's traditional Southern upbringing. It was definitely more brash and confrontational, but not unfamiliar to me.

"Did you think that about me when we first met?" I asked. "That I was a little pushy, but I meant well?"

Reluctant to take her eyes off the stop-and-go traffic, she glanced at me then back at the road again. "Tommy, when I met you, I thought, 'Well, here is a charming young man who knows how to flatter and charm a woman and look at her in a way that makes her feel like there's no one else in the room.'"

"Hm," I hummed with a chuckle. "That obvious, huh? I thought I was being subtle and respectful."

"You were," she said, then corrected herself. "You are always respectful. Subtle, never. But always respectful. It's flattering to get that kind of attention from a young man. Especially when you've spent a majority of your life married to a man who seemed determined to trade you in for a new and improved model." Her mouth flattened into a bitter line.

"I'm sorry."

She scoffed. "I'm not. He cheated on me for years. I wish I didn't have to deal with the remnants of his affair, but—" She drew in a sharp breath and cringed. "I'm sorry. I shouldn't have said all of that."

"No...it's fine. It's not as if we haven't talked like this before."

"I know, but it's not something I want to dredge up right now. Jared's getting married. This is a happy occasion."

"Understandable. But just know that I'm ready and willing to be a listening ear. I'm just sorry you had to go through all of that. You deserve so much better, Darcy."

When I said her name, she looked at me again. A sad smile curved her lips. "You're a sweetheart for saying so."

She pulled her car into the valet space in front of the hotel. I signaled to the valet to give us a minute, then turned toward Darcy in my seat. "So, the funny thing about sharing calendars is that I can see yours too. As it turns out, I'm not the only one in need of a little vacation."

"I live in Charleston. When the weather's warm, I can take a trip down to the beach whenever I want."

"Except you don't."

"You're right," she agreed. "I don't."

I nodded. "When we were driving in from the airport, Jared asked me to take care of you this weekend—"

"Seriously? Don't listen to that boy. I'm fine. You're here to enjoy yourself—"

"Darcy, taking care of you and making sure this weekend is just as memorable for you as it will be for Jared would be enjoyable for me."

Her eyebrows arrowed upward over her sunglasses. "Are you sure about that? Our schedule seems to be pretty tight." She tipped her head in the direction of her mounted iPhone that had just thrown up a reminder to 'meet the guys at the hotel bar for drinks.'

"I made the schedule, Darcy. I can make time."

Now she turned toward me in the seat. "What exactly are you suggesting here?" she asked.

"Exactly what I said. Let me take care of you this weekend. Let me be your plus-one. I'll keep your glass full, spin you around on the dance floor, and keep that smile on your face."

Because she was smiling now, and it was a gorgeous thing to see.

"That's really sweet but so unnecessary. I don't need you to do all that."

"Excuse me if I'm being too bold, but I'm not sure you even know what you need anymore. Like I said at the restaurant, I think you deserve to have your needs catered to."

"By you? You think you're the man to do that, huh?" she asked sarcastically. But I heard a note of curiosity and maybe a whisper of desire in there, too. I might have imagined that last bit but that didn't matter if I could keep that smile on her face and that blush in her cheeks.

"Darcy..." I said with a sigh and shake of my head. "I'm absolutely the right man."

Her lips parted on a tiny, soft gasp, and I couldn't keep the smile that felt borderline feral from stretching across my lips. My phone jangled the tune dedicated to schedule reminders. I pulled it out, observed the alert, and silenced it. "Okay, it looks like you need to be at the dress shop for a final fitting, and I'm supposed to start getting drunk in the next five minutes."

I turned my attention back to Darcy, who still wore a look of surprise. I wanted to lean across the console and draw the tip of my tongue across her wet bottom lip before gripping the back of her neck and inviting her to do what she wanted with me. Instead, I took her hand, turned her palm upward, and kissed the thrumming pulse at her wrist.

"Just give it some thought, Darcy," I whispered before getting out of the car.

3

DARCY

The thin skin on the inside of my wrist tingled where Tommy's lips had touched as I watched him cross the sidewalk to the hotel lobby doors. On the list of things I'd thought Tommy Martinez might say, "Let me take care of you," wasn't among them. The suggestion seemed innocent enough at first. Sweet, if not slightly insulting. I was the one who took care of people. I planned the things, made sure everyone was fed, bedded, taken care of — I'd done that for him, in fact. But now, this young man that I'd fed at my table wanted to make sure I was happy, to make me smile through the difficult parts of this milestone weekend.

And the look in his eyes when he said it, the way his lips granted the barest of kisses to a place that was both innocent and intimate to kiss...

"Ha..." I coughed out the surprised sound as I finally tore my eyes from the door Tommy had disappeared through without so much as a glance backward. As if he knew that his words and actions had sparked a confused riot of feelings in my body.

I put the car in gear and pulled into traffic. There was a perfectly good explanation for the way my body reacted. It had been a while since I'd been touched so intimately. I was what people called a touchy-feely person. I liked to give and receive hugs. I was just as generous with my kisses. A good back rub could make a hard day or hurt feelings much better as far as I was concerned. I also liked to be kissed and held, but...there hadn't been much of that lately. I'd been deprived of that kind of skin-to-skin contact, and the absence of touch probably led to this full-body reaction from just a brush of his lips to the inside of my wrist. Pathetic, I know, but that was the only explanation that made sense.

That, and well... It would be pointless to deny that I've been having a hard time since the death and the public humiliation of my District Attorney husband's young mistress and son showed up at the funeral. I thought I would be done with this part of the grieving process by now, but I kept vacillating between anger and depression and back to anger again. With Jared in Chicago, it was easy to hide the worst of it from him. Or so I thought. I guess I couldn't be more wrong because my usually self-absorbed son was so worried about me that he asked his best friend to take care of me, so I didn't ruin his wedding.

And Lil' Tommy was all too willing and eager to oblige.

Maybe it was the fact that I hadn't seen him in damn near ten years, but Tommy as a confident, self-assured man knocked me for a loop. There had been a hint of that in his eyes on the cover of Architectural Digest, but it was altogether different to witness in person.

When Jared brought bright-eyed, ambitious Tomás Martinez home the first time, I was instantly charmed by him. He had a gracious way about him that went beyond good manners. The smallest gift or invitation resulted in the kind of supplication that made me uncomfortable sometimes. If I invited him to dinner — I had a lot of dinner parties back then — he would linger after the other boys went out to the pool to help straighten up and take out the trash. If we invited him to hang out with us at the beach in the warmer months, he would make store runs, schlep all of the beach equipment to and from the car, and just generally made himself useful.

We had a common love for historical architecture, and he would do tours with me if I was selling a house he wanted to see. And some nights — nights I was often alone — he'd sit by the pool, or in what he called my jungle room, and talk to me about any and everything until the wee hours of the morning. Tommy was deep, philosophical, and emotionally mature in a way I've yet to see in men twice his age. And I know that's a thing that people say when they want to make excuses for their attraction to a much younger person, but it really was true with Tommy. That year he lived in the garçonnière, I felt like we developed a sort of friendship. And sure... I had a fondness for him, and I knew that he probably had a crush on me. Sometimes he sought out my company a little too much — so much that Shannon had commented on it a time or two. And sometimes, the hugs went on a little long. But I never entertained the thought of anything sexual between us because, despite his emotional maturity, he was a boy. My son's best friend. His crush on me was never broached in a way that made it necessary for me to consider or confront it.

Now I wondered if my behavior had encouraged him in some way because here we were, years later, and he wanted to take care of me.

I gave that some serious thought as I slowed to a stop at a traffic light a few blocks away from the dress shop. Our late-night conversations came to mind. Innocent cuddling on the porch swing, a kiss on the temple, those long hugs. Shame set my ears and cheeks aflame. They may have been innocent, but after today's kiss, the memory of them felt...

A car horn behind me blared, startling me back into the

present. "Shit," I cursed softly, observing that the light was green. I flipped the driver the bird anyway because that was not a courtesy honk.

It was for the best, anyway. I had no business thinking about Tommy that way. Even if I could still feel his lips on my skin and remember how darkly suggestive his eyes were when he said taking care of me would be enjoyable for him. And I didn't need to acknowledge the fact that I'd noticed how much he'd filled out in the last few years. That he'd put on a bit of grown man weight, and the loss of that baby fat had leaned out his six-foot frame and chiseled his jaw, shifting him from handsome to fucking gorgeous.

"Jesus Christ, Darcy," I muttered to myself. *I should not be lusting over Tommy this way.*

But I had absolutely noticed all of that and more.

I parked my car on a side street and spent a majority of my two-block walk to the dress shop trying to cull my mind of the filthy thoughts about Tommy that were beating against the battened doors of my libido. I'd barely managed to rein them in when I stepped into the dress shop with my slingback heels dangling from my fingertips.

"Good Lord, Darcy!" my sister James exclaimed from her perch on the dais when she set eyes on me. "You're all flushed in the face. Did you run here or something?"

I touched my palm to my cheek and felt the heat there. "It's hot as Hades out there," I said by way of explanation.

"That it is," Cora, the shop owner said around a mouthful of straight pins. "Leslie, dear, get Darcy a cold bottle of water and put her in that second dressing room. Her dress is already on the door," she instructed while giving me a wink.

Leslie led me to the dressing room and gave me a bottle of water. "If you need any help, sweetheart, just give me a holler."

"Thanks, Leslie." Once the dressing room door was closed, I

dropped my bag in the chair and slipped out of the breezy sundress I threw on to go to lunch with Tommy and my son. When I looked at myself in the mirror, I saw that more than just my cheeks were flushed. A dusky red splotch covered the center of my chest, and my nipples were hard and begging to be touched. The place between my legs felt hungry and slippery wet.

The heat didn't do this to me.

Tommy did.

I shook my head at my reflection. *No, this is not allowed.*

Screwing off the top of my bottled water, I immediately tipped it up and gulped down half of its contents, hoping but knowing it wouldn't cool me off. Frustrated that I couldn't push his suggestion out of my mind, I yanked the dress off the hanger, stepped into it hastily, then slipped on my shoes and exited the dressing room.

James glanced at me as I approached the dais and three-way mirror. My sister was nine years younger than my fifty-five years, but remaining single and child-free had kept her as young and fresh as the day she turned eighteen. I felt those years as I came to stand next to her.

"Woo, chile... I can't wait to get my hands in this hair tomorrow," she said, attempting to smooth my humidity-curled edges. "All that swimming has fried your hair, sis."

"I know. I've been thinking of changing the pool to saltwater—"

"Not to mention the fact that you're shrinking down to nothing," Cora interrupted as she pinched at the waist of the dress that she had just taken in a few weeks ago. "You're not sick, are you?"

I flinched at that and glared at her. "Why would you even speak that into existence? No, I'm not sick. I'm just stressed and not eating much while planning this wedding."

"And swimming like you're training for the Olympics," my sister added.

I rolled my eyes. "Y'all talk about my swimming like it's a meth addiction or something. "

All three women gave me a suspicious look.

"Is it?" Cora asked hesitantly. "The granddaughter of one of the ladies I know at church got hooked on that meth last year. She wasted away to nothing, ruined her complexion, lost her teeth and everything."

"Jesus Christ, Cora. I have all of my teeth. I'm not smoking meth. I'm just stressed, working a lot, and swimming a lot." These conversations about my weight were getting annoying, especially since no one asked me outright how I was really feeling. The swimming was helping me manage my stress and depression. I would tell them this if anybody bothered to ask.

"Well, in a few days, the wedding will be over, and life can get back to normal," Cora said as she began to pin the loose fabric, cinching the dress around a waistline that I had to admit had vanished more than I realized. "How is Jared doing? Is he nervous?"

"He doesn't seem so." I smiled at my reflection as I thought of how my son made a special trip home to tell me about the girl that he was sure was the one after knowing her for three weeks. I managed to convince him that he should wait at least six months. Six months to the day, he flew home again to tell me he was definitely going to propose and asked me to go ring shopping with him. In the end, we decided to re-purpose the diamond his father had given me. The setting he chose was his own design and beautiful.

"No, my nephew isn't the type to get cold feet," James said with a smile. "He's always been very decisive about what he wants, and this girl is no different."

I nodded and smiled. My son was a lot like me in that

respect. Loyal and faithful. Thankfully, he was better at choosing the right people to be loyal and faithful to.

"Is he staying at the house?"

"Yeah, in his old room, and his friend Tommy from college is staying in the garçonnière."

James rolled her eyes. "Why are you like this? It's an apartment over the garage."

"Garçonnière sounds more romantic," I answered with a sheepish shrug.

"Romantic..." James scoffed. "I would've thought you gave up on all romantic notions when Shannon died."

"Hey! You can't talk about infidelity on the eve of the wedding! Keep that bad energy away from me and mine."

"You're right," James said. The sentiment might sound superstitious, but she believed in it just as much as I did. "Wait... which one is Tommy again?"

Shit. More than just my cheeks heated this time, my whole body flushed. "You know...the one who stayed with me for a while when they were in college? He lives in Chicago, too. Owns an architectural firm there. Very successful. He was on the cover of Architectural Digest a few months ago."

"Oh, wow. I remember him now. He was a pretty one. So, he and Jared have remained close?"

"Very. Tomás is Jared's best friend, and he's his best man." Shame dampened the desire that had awakened inside of me when I saw that heated look in Tommy's eyes. I'd joked about taking a young lover at lunch, but I'd mostly done that to wind Jared up. In truth, it wasn't something I'd ever considered — not seriously, anyway. And not until Tommy pressed that kiss to the inside of my wrist.

But even if I did take a lover, my son's best friend was *not* an option.

No matter how beseeching those dark brown eyes of his were.

More than that, Tommy has always been a charmer. I was probably reading far too much into that exchange. Sure, it was a little flirty and suggestive, but it didn't mean he was really interested in me that way, right?

4

DARCY

After we left the dress shop, James and I walked up the block to have some drinks. We chatted about this or that until my phone started throwing off alerts for the rest of the errands I had to run. I met and paid the deposit for the band, swung by the caterers to make sure they didn't have any issues with my order, then headed back to the house to meet the guy with my liquor delivery.

"Hey, Darcy," Minerva greeted as I came in the back door. "You look flushed!"

"Everyone keeps saying that as if it's not hot out there," I muttered, hanging my bag on the coat rack in the mudroom. "Has Amos been by to deliver our liquor order yet?"

"He dropped off the spirits but had to double back to get the crates of champagne."

"Seriously? He did say he was coming back, right? I need that champagne for family brunch tomorrow."

"I'll give him a call," Minerva said, plucking her smartphone from the pocket of her practical dress. "In the meantime, have a seat. I'll pour you some lemonade."

"Make it a Lynchburg lemonade, and I'll pour for both of us," I said playfully.

The older woman winked. "I'll take a nip or two if you're offering."

"Oh, you'll take more than a nip, Minnie."

She chuckled huskily, shoulders shaking. "You know all my secrets."

"You know mine, too."

Minerva has worked for my family for as long as I could remember. When I got married and moved from Daniel Island into Charleston, Minerva "came with the house." I didn't really need a live-in housekeeper anymore, but Minerva wouldn't tolerate being fired. So, I've kept her on, and to be honest, she's the one who has helped me through some of the most difficult times in my life.

I went back out onto the side porch where the crates of spirits sat. Observing the boxes labeled Marrow Bone Creek, I opened the one on top and pulled out the bottle of locally distilled bourbon. I eyed the number of boxes and hoped it would be enough to keep these rot-gut Southerners drunk and merry for the evening.

Brunch would be just the immediate family, but the rehearsal would take place in the side garden tomorrow evening, and dinner would be served immediately afterward. I'd hosted many dinner parties over the years, but this was to be my first since the Shannon's death.

It was hard to pinpoint why I stopped having those dinner parties. Well, that's not entirely true. I was depressed; that much was obvious. And the shame around that depression made me self-isolate. I withdrew for so long that I felt a little like the girl who resurfaced after a night of horrible sex. Awkward and unable to participate in the vapid and insipid conversations I'd indulged in before because my life was so different now.

I'm different now.

So, I self-isolated again.

But when Jared flew into town with his brand-new fiancée on his arm and begged me to plan a wedding like one of my "old-school dinner parties," I couldn't say no. But in truth, I was dreading having all of these people in my house. Dreading the whispered conversations they would have in my home as I fed them and plied them with good liquor. The tension that thought caused in my shoulders made me want to rip my dress over my head and dive into the pool again. Instead, I took the bottle of Marrow Bone Creek into the kitchen, where Minerva was just hanging up with Amos.

"He's on his way back with four crates," she assured me as she took the whiskey from my hands.

"Good."

Minerva kept an old AM/FM radio on the counter in the kitchen; it was always tuned to the oldies station. I turned it on now, and Otis Redding proceeded to beg me to try a little tenderness.

Just as Minnie set a frosted glass of bourbon and cold, tart, homemade lemonade on the counter for me, I heard voices coming up the back path. Animated conversations between five boisterous young men crescendoed on the back porch. My son, already three sheets to the wind, stumbled across the threshold.

"Mommy! Minnie!" he said, throwing his arms wide. Behind him, Tommy, who wasn't completely sober either, shook his head and laughed as Jared wrapped an arm around both of us in turn.

"The band's back together, I see," Minerva said, her voice in that low, disapproving octave, and a smile in her bright blue eyes.

"Carter, Matthew, Scott, I know your mothers raised you better than to come into someone's home without giving them the greeting of the day," I said, looking at the flushed faces that had followed Jared and Tommy in.

"Hey, Ms. MacFarland. Hey, Ms. Minerva," they intoned in unison, and time slipped a little, swamping me with a strong sense of déjà vu. A memory of these same five boys in my kitchen on a Friday night when they were all in college.

"What are you boys doing here? I thought you'd be tearing up King Street until the wee hours of the morning."

"We would be, but Mr. Responsibility thought we should cut the evening short so we could save our energy for the bachelor party tomorrow night," Scott pointed at Tommy.

"I simply said that I have a pretty big evening planned for us, and maybe we shouldn't get shit-faced tonight. We have the fitting in the morning, and—"

"Oh, god. Please don't run that schedule down again," Jared complained. "Ma...do you have something in this house that will get this guy drunk?" he asked, gripping Tommy's shoulder.

"Well, me and Minnie just opened this bottle of Marrow Bone Creek—"

"Yes! That'll do it!"

Jared grabbed the bottle, brought it straight to his lips, and took three big gulps. I cringed as he grimaced, groaned, and passed the bottle to Tommy. Bleary-eyed, Tommy looked at the bottle with his brows furrowed.

"Don't be a pussy, Tomás!" Jared damn near bellowed.

"Yeah, drink or pass the bottle," Matthew cosigned.

"Fuck it," Tommy said, then tipped the bottle up.

As I watched him take three equally big swallows of the strong brown liquor, I resigned myself to the very real possibility of a long night of drunken, half-naked young men splashing around in my pool. And probably an early morning visit from the cops when my neighbors got fed up with all of the noise. Just like old times.

"Okay, I can see this is about to go sideways," I said. "Take it outside on the porch. And try to keep it down, okay? You know how Mr. Brothers likes to ruin a good time."

"Yes, ma'am," Jared said, smacking a kiss on my temple. "Can we grab a couple more bottles of this?"

"A couple means two, Jared. That liquor is for the reception."

"We'll keep it classy, Ms. MacFarland. I promise," Tommy said with a sly smile, and goddamn, the boy was stunning.

"Yeah... I'm sure you will," I said with a shake of my head.

"Hey, Minnie, do you think you can order us some pizza or something—"

"I'll take care of it," Tommy said, pulling out his phone. The rest of the boys filed out of the kitchen onto the side porch, unbuttoning their shirts as they went. He lingered, staring at his phone. "Who delivers here again?"

"Don't worry about it, Tommy. I'll take care of it," I said.

He looked up from his phone and frowned. "You didn't hear anything I said to you this afternoon, did you?"

"I don't see what that has to do with—"

"I said I'd take care of you this weekend, remember?" Before I could react, he swept me up into his strong arms and pressed his firm body against mine. "I promised I'd keep your glass full, spin you around on the dance floor..." He swung me out and twirled me around to demonstrate, and a sound came out of me. A delighted snorting laugh that I hadn't made in years. "...and make sure that smile stays on your face."

He leaned in a little too close. And when he leaned in... I felt myself leaning, too.

"Ahem!" Minerva coughed loudly, startling us apart like teenagers caught dancing pelvis to pelvis at the school dance.

Tommy glanced at her, a slightly annoyed look on his face. "I forgot you were even standing there."

"It happens," Minerva said with a shrug.

He handed me his phone with the food delivery app open. "Just order from the nearest pizza spot. I'll pay for it," he said, backing away slowly. "And we'll finish that dance later, won't we?" he asked, raising an eyebrow.

"Tommy, if you don't get your drunk ass out of my kitchen!"

"Is that a yes, or..."

I grabbed a wooden spatula from the container by the stove, and I swear, all of his playfulness fell away when I stepped in close, wielding it like I was going to whack him on the ass.

"Watch out... I might actually like that," he said, then bit his bottom lip in that seductive way pretty men did when they were thinking about kissing the fuck out of a woman.

"Sir! That was not an invitation. Get out there with your little friends. I'll order the pizza," I said, trying to keep it playful, but my voice was shaky, and when he dragged his gaze down my body, I felt it like it was his hand.

"Okay, I'll go play," he said with a smirk, then turned and walked out of the back door.

"And stay away from those wedding decorations. If I wake up to vomit on my lawn—"

"Come on, Darcy," he said, his smirk stretching into a full-on mischievous smile. "We're not a bunch of drunken college kids anymore. We can hold our liquor."

"Yeah, we'll see," I said, then watched him pull his shirt over his head, revealing a flat muscled belly with a fine dusting of dark hair that grew in even darker and thicker just below his navel.

I stood there for a moment, just dragging air in and out of my lungs and trying to calm down before I turned to Minerva. "How many pies do you think those boys will eat? Five? Ten?"

"I'd go with five," Minerva said, then chuckled as she reached for her glass of spiked lemonade.

"What?" I asked.

"That one has always been fond of you, hasn't he?" she asked with a knowing smirk.

I coughed out a nervous chuckle and nodded. "And too damn mannish, if you ask me."

"Hm. There is nothing mann*ish* about him now. He's definitely a grown man." The look on Minerva's face shifted into something more...lascivious? Yes, that was exactly what that look was, and I was scandalized.

"Minnie!" I gasped, giving her arm a playful thwack.

"Don't act like you didn't notice."

The laughter died on my tongue as shame set my neck and cheeks aflame. "Yeah, I noticed." And now, I was beginning to realize that it was a problem.

———

MINERVA and I did a quick inventory of the food and drink that we needed for tomorrow's brunch — the first of two I would host this weekend. This one was going to be small, close family only, but I was more nervous for it than anything else. Mostly because Jolene was going to be there.

Me and my husband's mistress haven't been in the same room in more than a year. Shannon willed her his portion of my business when he died, so we were business partners at MacFarland Brokerage, but that was in name and paperwork only. I ran the agency, and she was free to do whatever the hell she does without much interaction between the two of us. Jared was close with his little brother, but with him in Chicago, I only had to be comfortable with knowing he would visit his brother whenever he came into town. But tomorrow morning, Dylan would be in my house, eating at my table *with her*, and I'd be a liar if I said it didn't fucking bother me.

Maybe that was why my mind latched onto Tommy's charm

and boyish flirtation this afternoon. I knew that's all it was. I would be silly to read anything more into it.

I sent Minerva home, poured myself another spiked lemonade, and made my way upstairs.

I loved this old house.

It was a Charleston single, a popular floor plan that could be found in a variety of styles around the Holy City. Mine was a Victorian. In the last seven years, I'd made this house completely mine — leaned all the way into the eccentric plant lady moniker that my friends and family had so lovingly slapped on my back. I caressed my babies, stroked their leaves, and talked to them as I made my way to the stairs, stopping in the foyer to inspect my most prized possession, an eight-foot monstera deliciosa grown from a clipping my grandmother gave me on my wedding day. It was a family tradition, one I intended to continue by gifting Brandi a clipping once she and Jared said their I dos. I just hadn't decided which of her gorgeous leaves to clip yet.

"Hm... My marriage may have died on the vine, but you're flourishing, aren't you? My beautiful monster," I murmured with a sigh, then turned to climb the stairs to my bedroom.

Greenery crowded the upstairs hallway, making it seem more narrow than it actually was. The leaves created a buffer from the street noise, which was almost constant. I still heard the boys in the yard, though, their laughter cutting into the quiet and spinning me back through time.

In my bedroom, the doors of the piazza were open to the side garden, and now I could hear their conversation more clearly.

"Your mom..." Scott said. "She's looking mighty fine."

"Okay, enough of that," Jared grumbled.

"I'm just saying. She could still get it."

"He said that's enough," Tommy said, a sharp edge to his voice that made strange feelings stir in my belly.

"Oh, so you're the only one who can talk about his mama like that?" Scott asked.

Was he winding Tommy up intentionally? Quietly and carefully, I stepped out onto the piazza. It wasn't that I was angry about those quips from Scott, but...I did want to hear what Tommy had to say in response.

"First of all, I don't talk about Darcy—"

"Darcy?" Scott interrupted, his tone incredulous.

"Ms. MacFarland," Tommy corrected. "I don't talk to her or about her that way."

"Nah...you just turn into a panting little puppy whenever she comes into a room," Carter said with a laugh. "I mean, don't get me wrong. We've all had a crush on her at one time or another. But I thought you would get over that. It appears I was wrong."

I waited to hear Tommy make some sound of dissent, but none came. Instead, Scott said, "Oh, shit! Look at his face! You thought we didn't know you had a crush on her all this time?"

"Guys... I'm sitting right the fuck here," Jared complained.

"I'm just saying—"

"Shut the fuck up, Scott," Tommy snapped.

The group went quiet, and I knew that Tommy and Scott were exchanging one of those tense looks. I'd seen those looks more than once when they were younger. The group of young men gathered on the bottom floor piazza all called themselves friends, but it was clear who they were loyal to — Jared. My son had always been the center of the group, the one that brought all of them together. The four of them — Jared, Matthew, Carter, and Scott — all came from money. They met in preschool and remained friends all the way into adulthood. Tommy was the outsider, and Matthew, Carter, and Scott treated him that way. They hated that he and Jared were so close. Maybe that was why I always looked out for Tommy when he was around. Treated him special. Hell, part of me wanted to go down there and get between them now. End this petty disagreement and take Tommy into the kitchen for some cookies. But that was the exact reason why they were teasing him, wasn't it? My preferential treatment.

"You're fucking disrespectful," Tommy said in a low, dangerous voice. "I thought you would have grown out of that, but I guess not."

I heard the scrape of the chair as he stood up, and a few moments later, I watched Tommy's broad, muscular back stalk toward the pool and dive in.

Quietly, I stepped back inside and closed the piazza doors. They were grown men now. They could sort out their problems without me getting involved.

I took a quick shower, pulled on my favorite silk robe, poured myself another drink, and went back onto the piazza. Tired but still too wired to sleep, I decided to read until I was sleepy enough to climb into bed. The boys weren't arguing anymore. They'd taken to reminiscing in low voices, which I was glad of as I turned on my Kindle and cued up my latest steamy read.

The self-proclaimed bad boy millionaire had just told the pretty postulant that he'd wanted to fuck her since the moment he saw her when I heard it.

Retching.

Dropping my Kindle on the chaise cushion, I stood and leaned over the railing of the piazza, scanning my yard to find Matthew bent over my knockout roses, throwing up his whole life.

"Goddamnit, Matt!" I cursed. "Not my goddamn rose bushes!"

Cinching my robe tighter around my waist, I ran down to the side yard. Jared was snoring on one of the chaise lounges. I gave him a smack as I passed. Tommy was in the pool but swam to the edge and levered himself out of the water the moment he saw me.

"I thought you had this under control, Tommy?"

His face crumbled into such a heartbreaking look of contrition that I immediately felt bad for putting this on him. "I'm sorry. I'm so sorry. I'll take care of it." He was drunk, but not nearly as drunk as the rest of them.

Tommy ran over to the garden shed and grabbed the hose while I attempted to assess the damage from a distance. Unfortunately, that wasn't far enough away because the smell of regurgitated whiskey and pepperoni wafted toward me.

"Oh, god... Matthew," I complained, covering my mouth and nose. "If you ruined my knockout roses, so help me..."

"I'll get it cleaned up," Tommy said. He turned on the water and pointed it at the chunks of vomit, pushing it around instead of breaking it up.

I snatched it from him and rotated the nozzle to hard, direct spray. It broke up the chunks, and gradually, the smell started to dissipate. Thankfully, Matthew had stopped retching and was headed toward the garçonnière.

"Y'all's little reunion is over for tonight. It's two in the morning. Get yourselves to bed," I ordered.

"I'm so sorry, Darcy," Tommy said again as he took the hose from me, wound it up, and put it away. "Matthew has never been able to hold his liquor."

"You're right," I said with a laugh. "Stop apologizing. I shouldn't have put that responsibility on you. Everyone out here is an adult and should know their limits."

"I know, but I told you I would keep them in line—"

"It's fine. You fellas need to head to bed, though. Goodnight," I said then, on some inexplicable impulse, I leaned in to give him a kiss on the cheek. Just a kiss goodnight. Harmless. Innocent. Completely chaste...

Until he turned his head.

His lips brushed against mine. Hesitant but soft, with the slightest pucker that was barely a suggestion of a kiss. But my body registered it as one. My nipples furled against silk gone cold in the night air — reminding me that I was naked under my robe.

When the tip of his tongue, wet and hot, traced the curve of my lower lip?

I moaned...

But it was more than a moan. It was like the sound of a thing long-starved that had awakened at his touch. The tips of his fingers traced the lapel of my robe, and my pussy fluttered. The shock of it made me gasp his name in a sharp whisper.

"What are you doing?" I asked.

"Hmmm?" His fingers stilled, stopping just shy of my skin. He looked into my eyes. His were dark, deep pools of want that nearly pulled me in.

"Goodnight, Tommy."

He let out a long, slow, wistful sigh. "Goodnight, Darcy," he whispered.

I took a couple of steps back, feeling all the heat that our bodies had generated bleed away just as quickly as it had built. I shivered, and he saw it. The corners of his mouth twitched.

Aw, hell. I want to kiss him again. I wanted to lick the edges of that secret, wicked smile. Discover the taste of his mouth. Feel his wet, hot tongue circle my still hard nipples, split my slippery wet pussy lips, and fit around my aching clit. I folded my arms over my chest and backed up a couple more feet.

No. This was bad. Not good. Dirty. Wrong. *Bad.*

And I want it — want him.

Worse than wanting him? I was pretty sure Tommy wanted me, too.

5

TOMÁS

My first waking breath tasted like last night's whiskey. I stank of chlorine, sweat, and...was that pepperoni? "Oh, fuck," I grumbled, covering my eyes with my hand.

The drunken night I'd tried to avoid had happened, and in a spectacular fashion, if the conditions of my aching body and head were any indication. Hell, it felt like it was still happening in my head.

Like some frat boy, I'd allowed my college friends to bully me into getting shitfaced even though I knew the schedule we had to keep. Now, it felt like a tiny gnome with a pickaxe was hacking away at my temples, and I was just coming to the realization that I was lying in a wet bed.

"Wait..."

Did I top off this night by wetting the bed like a five-year-old?

Damn, I drank a lot in college, but pissing myself was not the end result of any of those drunken binges. Some brawls, and maybe some questionable sex partners, but...

Slowly and carefully, I opened my eyes just enough to look down the length of my body. I was still wearing the shorts I had on yesterday, but now they were dark and damp — thankfully, not just in the crotch. Gradually, memories of last night's activities began to filter through the hammering in my head.

The pool.

I'd jumped in the pool in my shorts and underwear after getting into a heated argument with Scott. And then I'd climbed straight into bed with them on.

That explained the sweat-and-chlorine stench that hung over my pain-wracked and dehydrated body.

Fuck...

Things weren't supposed to go this sideways. I was Mr.-Fucking-Responsibility. It was my job to keep these fools in line.

"God...where the fuck is my phone?" I groaned, levering myself out of the bed with nothing but sheer will to get me to my feet. The moment I stood up, my wet shorts tugged downward. I patted my pockets, but the phone wasn't there.

My internal clock told me that it was around eight or nine in the morning, so we hadn't overslept, but I needed my phone. I needed the exact time and the list of reminders of the errands and tasks I had to do. I tore up the bed, pulled out the nightstand drawers, got down flat on my belly to look under the bed and dressers.

The phone wasn't in here.

"Shit, shit, shit," I cursed under my breath while yanking the bedroom door open. "Haven't even been here a full twenty-four hours, and I'm already fucking up," I muttered.

Out in the living room, I found Carter, Matthew, and Scott sprawled across the sectional. They weren't invited to the family brunch, but they still needed to wake up so they could get back to the hotel to shit, shower, and shave before the tux fitting.

"Hey, assholes," I grunted, clapping my hands loud enough to crack my own skull. "Wake up. Time to get your asses back to the hotel to shower and change. We have appointments today."

"Martinez... I fucking hate you," Scott groaned, his face buried in the couch cushions. And honestly, that might be true. We were both here because we were friends with Jared, but we've never been tight.

"Now, you hate me. I told ya bitch ass not to get shitfaced last night. I knew this shit was gonna happen."

"Jesus Christ..." Matthew complained, rolling onto his back. "My mouth tastes like ass."

"Probably because you threw up a whole medium pizza last night," Carter volunteered.

My heart dropped into my shoes. "Matthew threw up? Where? Did you clean it up 'cause if I go in that bathroom and—"

"Relax, den mother. He threw up outside," Scott said. "Ms. MacFarland came out to handle it and sent us all to bed."

"Shit..." I cursed again, arrowing my fingers into my hair, which felt stiff and dry from the chlorine. "Was she pissed?"

"Nah...not really. She just hosed off the rose bushes. To be honest, she reacted as if she expected it to happen," Matthew volunteered.

I sighed in relief. "Good."

"She didn't get pissed until you kissed her. That's when she sent all of us to bed," Scott added.

My heart stalled in my chest. I turned to Scott, who was wearing a smug smile on his face. "I tried to kiss Darcy?"

"Who said tried?" Scott asked, pushing himself off the couch. "You did kiss her." He bumped my shoulder as he made his way down the hall to the bathroom. But I was too stunned by his words to react or retaliate.

I kissed Darcy?

Wow. That Marrow Bone Creek bourbon must be stronger than I remembered because I had no recollection of kissing Darcy. And I really wanted to have some recollection of kissing

Darcy. Even if it was drunken and sloppy and ended with her slapping me—

And now my dick's awake.

Scott stumbled out of the bathroom, still pulling up his pants. Matthew made movements toward the open door, but I shoved him back.

"No. I need to get ready, and the three of you need to get out."

"Come on! I just need to take a piss!" Matthew whined.

"Go to the main house. Piss in the alley. I don't give a fuck." I closed the bedroom door, stripped out of my still wet underwear and shorts, and stumbled into the bathroom. My dick bobbed out in front of me, hard and ruddy dark, pointing the way as I reached in to turn on the shower. While the water heated up, I looked at myself in the mirror. My eyes were bloodshot, and my face was covered in half a day's scruff, but I saw no bruises or welts, so maybe she didn't hit me. But fuck... I wished she had.

Part horrified that I had crossed that boundary without her consent and so aroused that my head was swimming, I stepped into the shower and stood under the waterfall of hot water. I closed my eyes, gripped my dick, and dug deep for some remnant of the stolen kiss.

I was already halfway drunk when we came in from dinner last night. Darcy was in the kitchen, looking flushed and dewy and wearing an indulgent smile as she welcomed us. We bickered about who was gonna buy the pizzas, and I pulled her into my arms, and god yes, I remembered how that felt. Her body was tight but soft in the places I liked my women soft — breasts, ass, hips. She'd laughed when I twirled her, and after that laugh, we shared a moment...an almost kiss.

But Scott wasn't in the kitchen then, so that wasn't what he was talking about.

That moment with her against my body was good, though.

So good. Good enough to have me tugging on my dick as I squeezed my eyes even more tightly closed, still reaching for the actual kiss, and—

"Oh..."

She was in the doorway wearing a long, black silk robe with colorful birds of paradise all over it.

Yes...that was it.

I could tell that the robe had been hastily tied because it slipped off of her shoulder, and she flashed one firm, smooth brown thigh as she descended the porch stairs and marched across the flagstone patio that surrounded the pool. Her hair was tied up in a silk scarf, exposing her long neck.

She'd scolded me. "Tommy, I thought you had this under control?" she'd said, pointing to Matthew bent over a bush at the far end of the yard retching.

That scolding had made me climb out of the pool and drag the hose out, which she'd snatched from my hands to spray the flower bed.

There were lots of apologies. Mostly from me. She'd accepted my apologies then leaned in to give me a kiss good-night, a kiss that was aimed at my cheek. Full of liquor and cock-sure, I'd turned my head at the last minute and...

"Oh, fuck..." I groaned. Was it shame that made me lean against the tile and start fucking my fist? That made every detail of the kiss flood my mind now? The soft gasp of surprise when our lips brushed. The way her entire body went rigid as if she wanted to pull away but couldn't. The taste on her lips, the sour sweetness of the homemade lemonade, and bourbon that I licked from her bottom lip.

Then she made another sound, pained, but hungry. And the look she gave me before she pushed me away? She wanted me. I saw it right there in her blown pupils and her wet lips.

I replayed that moment, again and again, my mind latching on to the what ifs.

What if she hadn't pushed me away? What if she took my hand and slipped it into the shadow where her robe split? High on the inside of her smooth thigh, just inches from her silken heat.

My breath came in raspy bursts as I imagined myself parting that robe to find her bare underneath it. And, *oh god*...her pussy. Was it shaved and soft to the touch? Or was it covered in soft hair, the same shade of chestnut brown laced with sun-kissed gold as the hair on her head? Was she wet when I kissed her? Would she let me lick those lips hidden beneath that silk robe, within the dark shadow between her thighs?

A soft thump out in the bedroom made my hand still on my aching cock. It was barely perceptible over the sound of the shower and my ragged breathing, but I opened my eyes and saw that the bathroom door was now open. Not all the way, but cracked just enough that someone could see in.

Did I leave that open?

Nah, I was fairly certain I closed it because I knew I was coming in here to jerk off, and I didn't want to be disturbed.

But now it was open...

I stepped out of the shower stream, wiped the water from my face, and stared at that gap between the door and the jamb. My first thought was that Scott had caught me with my dick in my hand. That he was recording this so he could embarrass me later when we were out because he was that kind of asshole. I was about to open my mouth to tell him that recording someone nude without their consent was a criminal offense when the person spying on me shifted just enough for me to see that it wasn't him.

A tumble of dark brown hair. A flash of tawny brown skin.

Darcy.

Darcy was the little spy at the door, hiding in the bedroom, watching me yank on my dick while daydreaming about touching her.

This was my fantasy. This was the exact scenario I'd imagined yesterday morning in that tiny airplane bathroom as it circled the airport. That she was watching me come for her because I *only* came for her. Only came when she wanted it.

I looked down at my dick. Still hard. Still in my hand.

There was a bottle of bath oil on the shower shelf. I grabbed it and poured a generous amount onto the tip of my dick. Turning to face the mirror, I could see her more clearly. She was still watching — a flush high on her cheeks, one long-fingered hand at her throat. Our eyes locked in that reflection. I bit down on my bottom lip to hide my smile and proceeded to give her a show.

One slippery tug with her watching already had me a lot closer to coming than I'd been a moment ago.

"Fuck, Darcy..." I whispered. "Is this what you want? To watch me come for you?" I shook my head and sighed. "I've been coming for you for years, hermosa..."

I may have imagined it, but I swear I heard her moan. A deep, primal, but distinctly feminine sound. Real or imagined, the sound made a shock of intense pleasure shoot up from my balls to the tip of my dick. Precum spilled over my fingers as I teased the tip in short, rough strokes, wanting to draw this out but needing to come now.

Now, now, now, I need it now.

Hesitantly, mostly because I feared that she left the moment I started talking to her, I glanced at the mirror again. She was still there, but her eyes were on my dick, and the look on her face... *Fuck.*

Her tongue darted out to swipe at her bottom lip, and just that tiny visual sent me right over the fucking edge.

"Shit," I gasped, and she gasped, too, as my cum hit the glass shower door. My head swam a little, and I used my other hand to brace myself.

By the time I caught my breath, Darcy was gone.

Somewhat sated and infused with a newfound self-confidence, I finished up my shower.

My, my, my, how the tables have turned.

I'd convinced myself that this thing with Darcy could never happen — that even the idea of it was dirty, wrong, bad, and that she would only ever see it as dirty, wrong, bad. Or maybe she still thought it was. Maybe the dirty, wrong, badness of it gave this whole thing a spicy bite that I knew would make it all taste and feel so much fucking better. Either way, a subtle suggestion from me that crossed the boundary from harmless flirting to *I will most definitely fuck you if given the chance* had her spying on me as I masturbated.

A few moments later, I went back into the bedroom to get dressed. I found the bed stripped of its sheets and a fresh set left folded at the foot. Sitting on top of that freshly washed and folded linen was my missing cellphone. The screen flashed. A schedule alert, probably. I picked it up and unlocked the screen. In addition to numerous schedule reminders, I'd just received a text message.

DARCY: *When you're...all cleaned up,*
there's coffee in the kitchen.
We should probably talk.

6

DARCY

I've lost my mind.

This was how it happened, wasn't it? People joked about menopause. About how you experienced extreme mood swings from happy highs to teary-eyed lows, but what about this vicious spike in my libido? Did it cause that, too? Because what else explained the fact that I watched Tommy get off in the shower while whispering filthy things meant for me to hear?

Is this what you wanted? To watch me come for you?

Was it? Because I watched with hungry eyes and a wet pussy, and I swear I don't know how I left that apartment without stripping out of my clothes and climbing into that shower with him. Instead, I was running back to the main house with sheets that smelled like his stink bundled against my chest.

How weird would it be to bury my face in this smell and make myself come?

Because that's what I wanted to do.

Oh, god. I'm losing it. I'm fucking losing it.

Matthew, Carter, and Scott were sitting on the back steps waiting for their rideshare. I hid my face from them and scurried into the kitchen, where Minerva had already started the grits and bacon.

"Hey, Minnie," I said, trying to keep my tone light and not at all like a woman whose aching wet pussy demanded to be satisfied right this instant. "I'm just gonna put Tommy's sheets in the washer. Can you get those boys a grub-cup? Grits, eggs, and some bacon to help soak up all the whiskey they drank last night. They need to sober up a little bit before their car gets here."

"Sure, but let me get that laundry for you, Dar—"

"I've got it, Minnie. Just make sure those three don't throw up on my back porch."

On bare feet, I speed-walked down the back hallway to the laundry room and slid the pocket door closed. Flipping the lock to engage it, I unbuttoned my jeans and slipped my hand down into my panties without giving it another moment's consideration.

Wet. So wet. Wetter than I'd been in years. I stroked two fingers over my clit and had to stifle my cry of pleasure against the sheets I'd dumped on top of the dryer.

I closed my eyes, and his face filled my mind's eye. Desperate need gave his features a severe look that made my heart and pussy throb. The way his forearm flexed with each slippery tug...

My pussy clenched around my fingers.

Is this what you want? To watch me come for you?

"Yes," I whispered, circling my clit with my wet fingertips.

I've been coming for you for years, hermosa...

My back arched as pleasure wound tighter and tighter. I buried three of my fingers deep, as deep as I could, wishing they were any part of him that my pussy clenched around as I came, muffling more cries into his dirty sheets.

"Shit," I whispered. This was fucking weird, maybe borderline deviant, but goddamn...

I wish I could say it was enough, but as I stood upright, bracing myself against the dryer on wobbly legs, I knew it wouldn't be.

But it had to be, right?

Disgusted with myself, I turned to the basin sink, and, grabbing the liquid soap, I scrubbed away the evidence of my orgasm. I had to get my shit together. And Tommy... We had to talk about this, get it out in the open, and nip it in the bud before it developed into something neither of us wanted.

———

THE REST of the family was due to arrive at ten, which gave me plenty of time to get everything done with Minerva's help. While she made pancakes, I went upstairs to change into another of my long bohemian dresses. This one plunged in the front and back and was a bit sexier than I usually wore to a family brunch. But there would be pictures, and I knew it photographed well. I contemplated putting my hair up again, but after playing around with it for a bit, I decided to leave it down. It may be dry and in need of a good trim, but I felt sexy and feral with it down around my shoulders and doing its own thing.

I put on a pair of wedge sandals and made my way back down to the kitchen, where Minnie was pulling a pan of biscuits out of the oven. I donned an apron and immediately got to work helping her spread butter and drizzle honey over them. We'd just finished up that task when Tommy walked into the kitchen.

My belly did a lazy flip when our eyes met, and he gave me that secret, wicked smile.

"Good morning," he said, his voice polite and as steady as his eyes were on me.

"Good morning, Mr. Martinez," Minnie said cheerily. "You want some coffee?"

"I'll get it for him, Minnie," I said, placing a hand on her shoulder. She gave me a sideways glance, because yes, I was acting weird and skittish. I needed to settle the fuck down.

"Cream? Sugar?" I asked, opening the cabinet and reaching for two mugs. When I turned toward him again with the mugs in hand, his eyes flicked upward, and he gave me a sheepish smile. He was checking out my ass, and now I was glad for all that stress management swimming.

"Just cream, please."

"No sugar, huh?"

"No... I think most people would agree that I'm sweet enough already."

You definitely are. I bit my lip to hide my smile as I filled both mugs with coffee and cream. I didn't take mine with sugar either. I handed him one of the mugs, and our fingers brushed, intentionally or unintentionally. Either way, that glancing touch made my cheeks flush, and I suddenly felt too shy to meet his eyes.

"Let's step out on the side porch and talk for a minute," I said, tipping my head in that direction.

"Okay."

Tommy walked out ahead of me, which gave me a chance to get a good look at him. He had become a damn good dresser, but money could do that for a man — and that's what he was, wasn't he? A man who knew that tailored clothes could make a casual collared shirt and shorts look expensive. That when a seam fell in just the right place, it broadened the shoulders and tapered the waist.

He turned to me, smiled, and gestured at the two Adirondack chairs. "Should we sit?"

"Uh...yeah," I stammered because now, he had caught me checking him out.

This part of the side porch got full sun in the morning, which was why I'd placed three big planters of elephant ears to create a little shade and some privacy from my neighbor's windows, which looked onto it.

"You look...amazing, by the way," he said softly. His eyes raked over my body and lingered at the plunging neckline for so long I wondered if I'd unintentionally flashed a nipple. But when I attempted to surreptitiously adjust the bodice, he whispered, "Sorry," then shook his head as if he were trying just as hard as I was to get his thoughts in order. "So... Thanks for returning my phone," he murmured, then looked up at me.

Is this flop sweat? Suddenly my top lip and the back of my neck, along with one much more intimate place, felt very moist. "Uh... Yeah. About that—"

"Don't apologize," he interrupted. "It's okay. It's more than okay. If anything, I should be the one apologizing."

"For what?" I asked.

"Last night? The kiss? I'm sorry about that, but you were standing so close, and you smelled so good—" He bit his lip and looked down into his cup again. "I'm making excuses. I took liberties. I shouldn't have done that."

"It's okay. It's more than okay," I said, echoing his words. "I think you know that I liked it."

A frown creased his brow, and he nodded. "And I think you know I liked you watching me this morning."

"God... This conversation isn't going the way it was supposed to."

"How was it supposed to go?" he asked.

"I was supposed to acknowledge that we're both feeling a sort of...pull toward each other. And then circle around to why we can't act on it. Except now, I'm just thinking..."

"Thinking what?" he asked.

I raised my head and finally looked him in the eye. "I'm just thinking about what you said and wondering if it was true."

"What? That I've been coming for you for years? Yes, Darcy. Yes."

That three-letter word...god, how did he make that three-letter word sound so filthy and suggestive? And years? Scott was right. He did have a crush on me — then and now.

I licked my lips and shifted toward him in my chair. "Listen... I think we both know that that this thing can't happen."

"This *thing*? Can you name it? Call it what it is? I...I think I'd like to hear it," he asked haltingly.

"That kiss last night...me watching you in the shower this morning. We can't let this go any further than it already has. You're my son's best friend, and I don't think you want to test your relationship with him in that way. We can't cross this line, Tommy," I whispered. I swallowed hard and realized that even talking about how we couldn't act on it had made me slippery wet. God, the wrongness of it, the wrongness of wanting him like this, made my hunger for it even more delicious.

"It's really hard to talk about a line we can't cross when what I want is on the other side, knowing that you want it, too."

"Tommy, you can't...we can't..." I looked around, afraid that someone overheard him. *God.* I really wanted to be kissed right now. *Needed* to be. "Jared would be upset and disgusted with both of us. And honestly! I'm old enough to be your mother—"

"I'm aware," he interrupted. "But you're not my mother." He set his coffee cup on the arm of the chair and turned toward me, making the space between us more intimate. "My relationship with Jared is important to me. I'm closer to him than I am to any of my brothers, and that's not something I want to lose, but...fuck, Darcy. I haven't been able to talk myself out of wanting you since I was nineteen years old. And after last night and this morning... I don't know how you can expect me to."

"Tommy, I—"

"Nope. It'll be impossible at this point." He shook his head and coughed out a laugh filled with complete disbelief. "Now that I've had a hint of your taste and heard your soft, growly, kitten moans? There's absolutely no fucking way that I'm going to be able to stop wanting to hear those sounds or wanting to be inside of you so—"

"Are you sure I look okay?" a familiar voice said just beyond the giant elephant ear leaves that hid us from view.

"Baby, you look perfect. Gorgeous. What are you so worried about, anyway?" Jared said. Brandi and Jared were coming up the back walkway.

"We should probably drop this subject for now. Or permanently," I said, then practically jumped to my feet. "Everyone will be here soon, and we can't... We shouldn't—"

Tommy tipped his head and gave me a pained look. "Darcy," he whispered.

And damn it, I should have never given him permission to use my given name because hearing it whispered from his lips made denying this dark, needy thing growing between us even harder to ignore.

He reached for me and grabbed my wrist in a loose hold, stroking the pad of his thumb over my pulse point. "Can we please continue this conversation later?"

"What would be the point in that?" I asked, trying not to be swayed by his gentle, reverent touch. "We can't have each other, so what's the point of talking like this?"

He let me go and sank back into the chair. "You're right," he murmured.

The look on his face damn near crushed me. "Tommy—"

"Hey, ma! And Tommy...what's going on?" Jared asked,

glancing between the two of us as he climbed the stairs with Brandi trailing behind him. "Everything okay?"

"Of course!" I said, pulling him into a quick hug and a kiss. "Just sharing a cup of coffee and some conversation."

"I was apologizing for letting things get out of control last night," Tommy volunteered.

Jared cringed. "Yeah, sorry about that, ma. We didn't cause too much damage, did we? I really don't remember much."

"Don't worry about it. Me and Tommy took care of everything. Brandi! Look at you! I love this dress, and your hair looks so pretty that way," I said, hoping to disparage the negative thoughts she'd voiced when she was coming up the back walk. She really was a gorgeous girl. Dark-skinned, and fine boned with big, upturned eyes, and tiny little chin that gave her face a doll-like appearance. I knew how it felt to have a mother-in-law who disapproved, and I didn't want to put her through that. Besides, she really was a lovely girl. I decided to make more of an effort to connect with her today. And it would be a good distraction.

"I love your dress, too!" Brandi said, a nervous smile playing on her lips.

I could feel Tommy's eyes on me as I escorted Brandi inside. It took everything in me not to return that look. To offer him some sort of comfort after the way our conversation ended. I knew he felt sore about it, but what could I possibly say to soothe him? Nothing I said was untrue. We couldn't have each other, so we both just needed to accept that.

"You know... I think it's officially mimosa o'clock. What do you think?"

An hour later, my parents, my sisters, and my in-laws had arrived, and I was trying my best to get everyone fed and situated.

"Well, I thought this was a sit-down breakfast," Lillian, my mother-in-law, complained as she stood in the buffet line that we'd created.

I was never really sure how to handle this relationship. *Are your in-laws still your in-laws when your husband is dead?* took a deep breath and barely refrained from rolling my eyes. "I can make your plate for you," I offered, attempting to be generous.

"No, thank you. I was just commenting on what I expected."

"I see. Well, I'm hosting a lot of things this weekend with very little help, so I figured a buffet was fine for today. I thought it would be nice to have a more intimate setting for family as well."

"Well, it's definitely intimate," the older woman groused, and I decided to leave the conversation there and grab another mimosa.

"Everything looks beautiful, Ms. MacFarland," Brandi said as she sat down next to Jared with her plate.

The table I'd rented for this brunch was covered with white cloths. The floral centerpieces were made with flowers from my garden, lilacs, and hydrangeas, mostly because Brandi said they were her favorite.

"Thank you, sweet girl," I said, and the smile I gave her didn't feel forced this time.

"Really, Darcy. You have a lovely home," Joseph, Brandi's father, said. "And a really beautiful garden."

"Absolutely beautiful," her mother Denise added. "But it seems like a lot of work."

"It is!" I agreed, coming around the table to sit next to Jared. "But I find gardening cathartic and soothing." I was just about to pull out my chair when Tommy appeared at my shoulder.

"I'll get that for you," he murmured, pulling the chair out for me.

Startled by his sudden closeness, I took a deep, steadying breath as I sat down. "Thank you, Tommy."

"No problem. I'm at your service this weekend. Remember?" He cupped my shoulder in a way that probably looked completely harmless to everyone at the table, but the feel of his hand on my bare shoulder sent a rash of goosebumps racing across the surface of my skin.

"At her service?" my sister James asked. "How does one sign up for this one-on-one service?"

"By the groom's request," Jared said before Tommy could respond. "Mom doesn't have a date for the wedding, so I wanted to make sure she had someone to look out for her. Who better than my best friend?"

When I planned the place settings for this brunch, I'd seated Tommy across from Jared because I figured that the two friends would want to chat. Now, I realized that it meant that he was sitting across from me, too, so that when he winked in response to Jared's statement, I saw it and the borderline lewd smile that curved the corner of his lips.

"Lucky girl," my sister Amelia said, a little tinge of judgment in her voice and with good reason. Keeping up appearances was important to Amelia, and attending my son's wedding without a date *just wasn't done*. She'd tried to set me up with numerous men leading up to this wedding, and I'd turned every one of them down. So the idea that my son's best man would be my escort definitely wasn't something she would be okay with.

"I told both of you that this is completely unnecessary. Frankly, I find the idea that you think I need to be babysat a little insulting."

"Don't think of it as babysitting," Tommy said, picking up his Bloody Mary. "Think of it as... Mother of the Groom Concierge Service. Here to assist, support, and satisfy your needs."

It wasn't unlike the flirting he'd always done with me over the years, so everyone laughed, but my cheeks went hot, and I had to avert my eyes because the idea of Tommy going above and beyond to satisfy my personal needs this weekend had me thinking really filthy things. "Concierge to the Mother of the Groom, huh? In addition to whatever best man duties you have, this weekend? Are you paying this man, Jared?" I asked, a weak attempt at making light of what felt like a suggestive statement.

"You've seen my schedule. Most of that stuff has been planned for months now. And aren't you the one who said, nay, demanded that I have some fun this weekend?"

"Babysitting your best friend's mom is not what most people would call fun, Tommy."

"Hmmm... I don't know, Darcy. Thinking of absurd things to say to make you blush feels like a lot of fun to me."

And then, right on cue, I did blush. "Behave, Tommy," I scolded lightly.

"What's the fun in that?" he asked.

Mrs. MacFarland, Shannon's mother, cleared her throat, and thankfully, that was enough to douse the heat that Tommy was stoking between us.

"Where's Jolene? She did say she would bring Dylan, right?" Jared asked.

"They're probably just running. He'll be here soon." I gave his forearm a reassuring squeeze. But that was a lie, wasn't it? Jolene had RSVP'd, but I had no idea if she was running late or had decided not to attend.

Dead for damn near seven years, and I'm still covering for him.

Tommy cleared his throat to draw my attention and gave me a questioning look. I gave him a subtle head shake. This weekend was not about Jolene or her affair with my husband, and I refused to make it about them.

"So, Tomás," my sister Amelia began, leaning forward so she could look down the table at him. "When was the last time you were in Charleston? Seems like it's been a while?"

"It has. Hm. I think the last time I was in town, you were

pregnant with your first kid," he said, gesturing toward my younger sister's pregnant belly.

"Oh, well, it's been a while then," James responded. "This one is her fourth!"

Gradually, the group at the table began to make idle conversation. Surface deep, but pleasant enough considering the group I had gathered here. Another hour more, and—

"I hope y'all didn't eat all the bacon!" Jolene bellowed as she came around the corner.

I was almost instantly annoyed by her presence. I couldn't decide what was worse — showing up late or not showing up at all. Once I saw her, that decision fell solidly into the showing up late column.

Shannon cheated on me pretty much the entire marriage. There was a time when I thought it was just something I had to endure. Men like him, men with massive egos and just as much ambition, needed more than one woman — or so I'd been told. And I guess I sort of made my peace with that in the early years.

Then he took up with her. Jolene Kirkland.

How ridiculous was it that her name was actually fucking Jolene?

She a younger version of me. Tall, fit, brown-skinned, half my age, and determined to be wife number two.

I spent more years than he deserved fighting for my marriage before he died. I'd actually come to the conclusion that we should get a divorce just before he had a heart attack. That should have been the end of it, right? Oh, but it wasn't because now, Jolene Kirkland was attending my son's wedding, and that just seemed un-fucking-fair.

Jared stood up and made his way around the table to greet Dylan who ran at him full tilt and leaped into his arms. The little boy favored him so much that it made me uncomfortable.

It was as if Shannon had tried to cut and paste himself into a younger version of the family he already had.

"Hey, Jojo," he greeted the other woman with a hug and a kiss while holding Dylan close to his side. "You remember Brandi," Jared said, pointing to his wife-to-be, who smiled awkwardly.

"I sure do. It's good to see you, Brandi." Jolene's eyes landed on me, and something like surprise flitted through those brown eyes of hers.

"Darcy..." she said, making his way to the only empty seats at the table, which unfortunately were at my end. "You're looking well." She came around the table to greet me and I stood so that we could exchange an awkward embrace and a kiss on the cheek. Why she felt compelled to do that, I didn't know.

"Thank you, Jolene," I said with a tight smile.

"Jojo," she corrected as if it wasn't incredibly infantile to be called a name better suited to a kid in pigtails.

"Right," I said with a toothy grin, feeling mean enough to bite. "Did you get caught up at the office? Brunch started hours ago."

She gave me a sheepish grin as Jared pulled out her chair. "You know how it is."

"I sure do."

"Mom..." Jared warned in a soft voice.

"I'm sorry," I apologized under my breath. "Excuse me, y'all," I said, standing up from the table. Tommy made as if to rise from his seat, and I dismissed him with a little wave. "Don't get up. I'll be right back."

"Is that Thomas Martinez?" I heard Jolene squawk as I made my way inside.

All of the doors and windows on the bottom level were open to catch the breeze coming off the river. I moved through those rooms to a space that I've always found calming in my home.

Damn it.

I thought that I was entirely over this. I thought I was entirely done with letting Jolene wind up my feelings like this. And this was just the pre-wedding brunch. How was I going to make it through this?

7

TOMÁS

W as Jolene Kirkland this narcissistic and annoying the first time I met her? If so, I didn't remember it. She showed up two hours late to the pre-wedding brunch, and from the moment she sat down, she was loud and dismissive of everyone at the table.

"Thomas!" she said between deep swallows of the mimosa Jared had made for her. "I saw your article in The Architectural Digest. That little firm you started after quitting your job at Edgewater Associates has worked out for you, huh? Looks like all of that idealism you've been married to since college is beginning to pay off."

I clenched my teeth at the purposeful mispronunciation of my name and said, "Yes, it is," because that was the only thing I could say in response to that thinly-veiled insult. "I wasn't aware that you knew anything about my firm or me for that matter."

"Of course, I do! Shannon talked about you all the time. Whenever you would come up in conversation he'd always say, 'that boy would go a lot further if he'd abandon all that that bright-eyed optimism'."

Hm. My grandmother always said that we shouldn't speak ill of the dead, but I think she would make an exception in this case because Shannon MacFarland was an asshole in life and apparently in death as well. Even worse, he was a specific kind of asshole, who ran for office campaigning on diverse issues, but still played into respectability politics in his everyday life. He'd often chided me about my ideas on slowing the gentrification of blighted areas, called them idealistic pipe dreams. I couldn't help feeling smug about turning those idealistic pipe dreams into some of my favorite projects as a developer and architect for my own firm.

"Well, congratulations, Thomas. There's something to be said 'bout sticking to your core beliefs and shaping your life and work around them. That's no easy feat for a man in this day and age. I applaud you for that."

"Thanks... I guess," I murmured. I glanced at the doorway Darcy had disappeared through. She'd been gone for a while now.

"Don't worry about her," Jolene said as if he'd read my mind. "You know she's always tended toward the dramatic."

I frowned and looked across the table to gauge Jared's reaction. He rolled his eyes, as if to agree that her statement wasn't remotely true, but didn't defend his mother either.

Not cool.

Pushing my chair back, I stood slowly and smoothed my hand down the front of my shirt. "I've never known Darcy to be the dramatic type, but even still, I feel it's within my duties as Concierge to the Mother of the Groom to see about my charge," I said, giving a dramatic bow before leaving the table.

"Concierge to the Mother of the Groom? What the hell is he talking about?" I heard Jolene ask as I stepped inside the cool, dim house.

Every window on the bottom floor was thrown open to catch the breeze off of the Ashley River. The air was cool and balmy, yet still a little sticky with humidity, in a way that felt pleasantly tropical and was distinctly Charleston. I stood in the hallway and enjoyed it for a moment. This was what came to mind when I thought of this city. That and this jungle house packed with house plants and Darcy with a spray bottle in hand, talking to them like they were people as she watered them.

Was that what Jolene meant when he said Darcy tended toward the dramatic?

Because when I looked back on it now, I wondered if all of that was just to mask how lonely she felt.

I moved through the dark, quiet house, passing her prized monstera deliciosa in the foyer, turned left at the stairway, and found Darcy curled into the fetal position on her chaise in her office.

"Darcy," I whispered.

She sat up abruptly and pushed her hair out of her face. "Is everyone finished eating? Let me get in the kitchen. Minnie is going to need help getting everything cleaned up."

"Relax, honey," I said, applying gentle pressure to her shoulder until she rested her back against the chaise. I sat at the end of the chaise near her feet. "The guests are fine. Everyone is still eating and drinking. I just came to check on the hostess."

"Oh...that's right. Mother of the Groom Concierge," she said, then laughed humorlessly. "I'm sorry if I made a scene. It's been a long while since I've been in the same space with Dylan...and Jojo," she explained. "I just needed a minute."

"That's totally understandable, and you didn't make a scene," I said, tracing my fingers down the length of her bare arm. Darcy sighed and grabbed my hand, lacing her fingers through mine. "Did I forget that Shannon was such a narcissistic asshole, or is that one of those things that become more obvious with distance and age? I can't imagine a man of substance dealing with the likes of Jolene."

She gave me a genuine laugh then. "To be honest, he was an asshole, but only with everyone else. He was more caring and loving with me and Jared. Well... he was until he wasn't."

I shook my head. "The way she says he talked about me...I can't believe I ever found him interesting and inspiring. Now he just sounds like all the rich white men I network with — bloviating endlessly about topics that no one but them care about."

"Unfortunately, that's exactly who he was." She sighed and stretched her long legs.

"Are you sure you're okay?" I asked, noting the way weariness had dragged down the corners of her mouth. I knew I shouldn't think this or say it out loud, but thank fuck that man was out of her life. I could see how he would have worn her down if he hadn't died and she'd stayed in that marriage. She deserved so much better than that.

"Yeah, I'm okay," she said with a nod. "I'll be fine. I just need to come to terms with the fact that I have to share this monumental event in my son's life with that vapid, arrogant woman."

"Well...whenever you feel like you need a break or you're worried that you might want to do murder, come find me."

She chuckled softly. "You don't have to do that, Tommy. Especially after our conversation earlier—"

"Shh..." I quieted, giving our interlaced hands a squeeze. "I agreed to do this before all of that. Seeing you in action at breakfast and this morning and realizing the lengths you go to make sure everyone is taken care of and how it goes completely unnoticed..." I shook my head. "I'm kind of ashamed of myself for being one of those people who treated you like that was something unremarkable. I'm so sorry, Darcy."

"You've always been so sweet to me. Underneath all of the ridiculous over-the-top flirting, you have always been such a sweet, sweet boy," she murmured, her light brown eyes searching my face. "But you're gonna have to knock it off before people begin to think you have real feelings for me. I think my sister James already suspects something."

I laughed and looked down at our linked hands, our entwined fingers. "Should I be ashamed that people know the truth about how I feel for you, querida?"

She shook her head and blushed hard. "What am I gonna do with you, Tommy?" she asked, her voice a husky whisper.

I shrugged. "Make a list of the things you want and need me to do, and I'll do my best to fulfill it in the seventy-two hours I'm in town."

"Tommy... You have to stop," she scolded.

"I'll stop if you really want me to, Darcy. Like I said, I'm at your service this weekend. I will do any and everything you ask of me. Whatever you want. I can be discreet. No one has to know what happens between us."

She parted her lips to speak but then closed them and gave me a contemplative look. Then, as if she came to some decision, she leaned in a bit closer and said, "What if I said I would give this some thought?"

Her voice had dropped into that low, sultry octave, saying those words that made my belly lurch excitedly. "I'd say—"

Both our phones started jangling alert tones. Irritated, I dug mine out of my pocket, and she did the same.

thirty minutes to tux fitting. Traffic is moderate to heavy. If you leave now, you will arrive at three thirty-one.

"Shit," I cursed under my breath as I stood up. "I don't want to leave this conversation unfinished again because something tells me the offer will be off the table if I do."

Darcy looked up at me and smiled. "Probably," she answered honestly. "What else is on your schedule?"

I thumbed open the schedule I'd set:

- *3:30 p.m. tux fitting*

- *check car and hotel reservations for Bran & Jay's honeymoon*
- *make sure J has picked and purchased his pre-wedding gift for B.*
- *double-check suite reservations, food, and strippers for the bachelor party*
- *5:00 p.m. rehearsal*
- *6:00 p.m. rehearsal dinner*
- *10:00 p.m. bachelor party*

For the first time in my life, I hated my ability to plan everything right down to the minute in order to get maximum productivity out of my day. There was no fucking wiggle room in this schedule. Doubly irritated now, I selected the rideshare app to call a car for me and Jared and sent a text to the guys at the hotel to make sure they were headed to the tux shop too.

"I... Maybe we can snag a moment during the rehearsal dinner?"

She stood and faced me with a sad smile on her lips. "This weekend isn't supposed to be about me, Tommy. We shouldn't be sneaking around during Jared and Brandi's rehearsal dinner to weigh the pros and cons of acting on feelings that we have no business feeling."

"Darcy." I moved in as close as I dared. "There are absolutely no cons to having this conversation. I will find the time."

"You can't just create more hours in a day, Tommy," she said, laughing at what probably sounded like a borderline tantrum to her ears. "This schedule is packed. Maybe that's the universe's way to prove to us that we shouldn't do this."

"I don't accept that," I said. "What about after the bachelor party?"

Darcy's brow creased with a frown. "After? I assumed that it would go on until dawn."

"Yeah, but it's in a strip club, which means — theoretically — that I could end the night when the lights come up."

"Really?" She arched an eyebrow and looked down at her phone to read the details on the itinerary. "You're going to leave a bachelor party with six strippers to come back here and talk to me?"

"There's a shit-ton of things I'd rather do than babysit a bunch of drunk frat boys, Darcy." *You, for instance.*

"And is one of those things old lady shit like drinking bourbon, while watering my plants, and gliding around my empty townhome in a caftan like a boo hag until dawn?"

"Wait, am I supposed to let the boo hag ride me in this version of the story, or—"

"Tomás!" Darcy squeaked then laughed until she was red-faced at my vulgar joke.

This was all I really wanted. To have her leaning into me, her laughter reverberating through both of us so that I couldn't help but laugh with her. While she was still laughing, I slipped my arms around her.

God. She smelled good and felt even better.

Gradually her laughter died down, and she looked up at me but made no move to step out of my embrace.

"Tomás Martinez, if I didn't know you better, I would swear you were trying to cop a feel."

"Hmm, I would say that you know me very well." I pulled her even closer so that she could feel what holding her this way did to me. "I am absolutely copping a feel, Darcy MacFarland."

"Jesus, Tommy," she whispered, dropping her head on my shoulder. She growled one of her soft kitten growls, and my dick throbbed where it was pressed against her belly at the sound. When she looked up at me this time, her lips were parted, pupils blown, giving me all the signs that she wanted to be kissed, and I was barely able to resist it.

"So…if you're still rambling around when the bachelor party is over, I'll come back here, we can have a drink and talk?"

Darcy sighed. A soft sound of surrender. "Okay," she agreed finally.

I bit my lip in a feeble attempt to hide my giddy smile. "Good, great—"

"Tomás!" Jared called, his voice trailing down the front hallway and making Darcy slip out of my embrace. "Mom? Is Tomás with you?"

"Yeah! We're in my study!" she answered, grabbing my hand to drag me out into the hallway behind her.

"Ah, good. My phone just told me it was time to head to the tux shop."

"Yup, I already called the car. It'll be here in three minutes," I said.

"You're so fucking efficient," Jared said, hooking his arm around my neck. Before brunch, I suggested that he should drink a couple of mimosas to take the edge off of his hangover. It appeared that he took me up on that…and then some.

I could only imagine the condition the other three in our crew were in.

Actual dread filled me when I thought about the bachelor party and how it was going to be more of the same shit that went down last night but with strippers and probably a few illegal substances.

Fuck.

But now, at least, I had the promise of seeing Darcy when these drunk fools finally passed out, and that gave me something to hold onto.

8

DARCY

In the few hours between sending everyone home from brunch and getting things ready for the rehearsal dinner, I managed to lubricate my bones and my attitude just a touch, but not too much. My sisters and I lazed about on the piazza with hand fans, shooting the shit in a way that we haven't had an opportunity to do in ages.

"Brandi seems like a nice girl," Amelia said as she swung her swollen feet into my lap and wiggled her piggies — a silent overture to have her feet rubbed, which I obliged.

"She is!" I said with a bit too much enthusiasm, but the bourbon probably had a lot to do with that. "I haven't spent a lot of time getting to know her. It's hard with them living so far away, but I plan to make more of an effort once they're back from their honeymoon."

"Where are they goin' again?" James asked.

"I got them a week in the Grand Caymans."

"Wow. Mama and Daddy only sprung for a four-day weekend on Tybee Island," Amelia grumbled with a tiny twinge of bitterness.

"Well, Jared's mama has more than enough money to do

something twice as nice for him and his new wife," I countered. "And he's my only son, so I will always go above and beyond for him."

"Amen to that," James said, raising her glass of bourbon.

"How are you feeling about all this?" Amelia asked.

"All of what?"

"I don't know... It's a big transition, your kid getting married and going off to start a family of his own. Does it make you wish you had more children?"

My gut clenched. I loved my sister, but I swear she could be petty and manipulative in the worst ways when she felt like she'd been slighted. She dug around and found the place she knew would hurt the most and poked it until she got the reaction she wanted. Knowing this, I bit back the urge to defend myself.

"If it were up to me, I would have. But to answer your question, I'm having mixed feelings about all of this." I stopped for a moment to sip my drink and find the words to describe what I was feeling.

"I'm happy that Jared has fallen in love and found someone that he wants to spend his life with. I'm excited for a whole new set of milestones and adventures that I can experience with him and through him. And grandbabies... I'm excited to have some of those, too. But..."

When I paused this time, it wasn't to take a drink. It was to swallow back the tears that had been building since my son told me he'd found the girl he wanted to marry.

"It just isn't happening the way you thought it would," James finished for me. "That's not your fault, Darcy."

"I know, but it doesn't make it hurt any less," I whispered. "Ugh, why the fuck did you make me talk about this, Amelia?"

"Because you never talk about your feelings, Darcy. You just keep 'em bottled up inside, and that's just not healthy, you know. Bottlin' up your emotions can cause cancer."

"Amelia!" James snapped. "Do your thoughts pass through any sort of filter before they come out of your mouth?"

"Shit, Darcy, I'm sorry!" my little sister said, wide-eyed and apologetic. "It happened so long ago that I forget sometimes."

"Sure." I didn't believe that for one minute. The reason why Jared was an only child was directly tied to her remembering that I'd had cervical cancer. She knew what she was doing, but I wasn't going to waste time arguing with her either.

Like a lifesaving beacon, my phone began to dance and vibrate on the table.

wedding rehearsal at 6:45

"Wow, everyone will be here in a few for the wedding rehearsal. Those couple of hours flew by, huh? I'm gonna go upstairs and freshen up." I pushed Amelia's feet off of my lap and stood up.

"Darcy, really, I didn't mean to—"

"It's fine, Amelia," I called over my shoulder.

But it wasn't fine. Yes, I was blessed to have all of the things I had: parents that were able to pay for my education, a beautiful and intelligent son, a reputable business, a historic home, and the money to send my son and his new wife on a seven-day Caribbean honeymoon. And yes, I was grateful for those things, but I was also acutely aware of the things I didn't have. Those things probably seemed like minor inconveniences to Amelia, who was pregnant with her fourth child and had a doting husband, and James, who was a self-proclaimed spinster who had no desire for either.

I sighed and closed the door to the master bathroom behind me. It was warmer up here on the second floor but not unbearable. Leaning over the sink, I checked my makeup. My foundation had started to break down a little bit, so I grabbed a few blotting papers to take care of the shiny spots and went over my whole face with a blending brush. My phone jangled and vibrated in my pocket, but it wasn't a scheduled alert this time, so I pulled it out to see who it was.

A voice text from Tommy. I pushed play.

"Hey, um. I don't know if this is out of bounds, but I just wanted to let you know that the moment that reminder for the rehearsal dinner came through, I thought about sitting with you in your study and holding your hand. And you with that look on your face like you wanted me to kiss you. Did you want me to kiss you? I should have just asked. Was that a missed opportunity?"

Yes, I'd wanted him to kiss me. Standing in the center of that space that always made me feel so calm and grounded with his arms around me and his hard length pressed into my belly as he whispered in my ear... Yes, I'd wanted that kiss. To be honest, I still wanted it. Wanted it just as much as I listened to him sigh in frustration about that missed opportunity.

"I hope...no, I need to know that I'll get that opportunity again, Darcy. And when I said that you should make a list of things you want me to do to and for you? I was serious." He chuckled and then sighed again. "I'll see you in a few," he said, then ended the message.

Then, like a lovesick girl, I played the whole thing again then saved it instead letting it disappear. Hm. This may be wrong. It may just be a thing that shouldn't happen, shouldn't be done. But there was no questioning the fact that the message from Tommy made me forget the bullshit. Without a second thought to how pathetic that was, I shoved my phone back into my pocket and went back downstairs.

———

PASTOR EVANS WAS the same minister who married Shannon and I and baptized Jared when he was twelve. My son thought it would be romantic to be married by a minister that had such a deep history with our family when anyone else would have seen it as a bad omen to be married by the same minister as their estranged parents.

Bless his heart.

"Mrs. MacFarland—"

"Ms.," I corrected, maybe a bit too harshly. "It's Ms. now."

"Oh, yes. Right," the pastor said with a solemn nod. "I haven't seen your beautiful face in our pews as of late. You're looking well."

"Thank you, Pastor Evans! And yeah, I've been attending Music of Life. Shannon and his extended family have always had Our Lady of Mercy as their church home, and I just thought it would be easier if it stayed that way. I didn't want to cause any problems." Shannon and I may have been married for years, but his family had never been very welcoming to me. I didn't see a need to continue to perform niceties once he was gone.

"Totally understandable," he said with another solemn nod. "So, Jared's getting married. Time really flies!"

"It sure does." We were standing next to the self-serve bar, and I took this moment to make myself another drink — whiskey neat because why even bother playing around at this point? Two more days of this painful small talk. Fucking torture.

Then Tommy's fine ass stepped through the French doors onto the lower level piazza with Jared and the other boys in tow. He searched the yard, and when his gaze landed on me, he gave me a smile that I felt between my legs.

"Oh, look! There's Jared now. Come here and say hello to Pastor Evans, son!"

Jared greeted the Pastor, then found Brandi and roped her

into the conversation. Tommy gave me a wanton look that paired well with his smile and pulled me aside.

"You saved my voice text," he murmured.

"I liked your voice text. Of course, I saved it," I whispered back.

"Oh," he said softly, a surprised yet bashful look on his face. "Is this bourbon?" he asked, pointing at my glass.

"Yeah, you want me to make you one?"

"No, it's hot out, and I've probably had enough already between brunch and the tux shop. I'll take a sip of yours, though."

With a smirk, I passed him the glass, and when he took it, he let his fingers brush against mine on the chilled glass. Why was that so fucking erotic? Holding hands, brushing fingers, long embraces... It felt like I was in a movie set in the antebellum South, and Tommy had come a-courtin'.

Well, sorta... Except for the fact I was a fifty-five-year-old Black woman, and he was a thirty-two-year-old Mexican-American, but it felt soft and sort of innocent in the dirtiest way possible.

"So..." he began while slowly bringing my glass of chilled bourbon to his lips. "Did you start that list yet?"

Now it was my turn to blush and look bashful. "Not yet, but I've been giving it some thought."

"Hm," he hummed, holding the bourbon in his mouth for a moment before swallowing. "You know I meant an actual list, right?"

"An annotated series of actionable items? Or will a bullet-pointed email do?" I asked.

"Either, but I want you to make it and send it to me. I like lists. I like instruction. I do well with directions. Very well." His lips quirked into a secret grin. "Should I keep an eye out for it?"

"Um..."

I looked around us at the members of my family and the wedding party milling around my yard. Could they see the attraction between us? Because it felt as real and physical to me as a hand on my pussy.

"How detailed do you want me to be?" I stammered.

Tommy could barely contain his glee as he stepped in close enough to place a hand on my hip and whisper in my ear. "All of them. All of the fine lines, the hash marks, and the layers that hide beneath them. Every secret you've ever kept and every Fibonacci sequence it will take to unlock them. I want all of the details, Darcy. All of them." He placed a quick, secret kiss on my neck. "Now laugh like I just said something hilariously lewd," he said, squeezing my hip before he backed away.

"Tommy!" I gasped in feigned surprise and gave him a little shove.

He stumbled away from me, putting on a wolfish grin. "I'm just sayin', whenever you're ready, we can play Me & Mrs. Jones."

"Wow, Tomás," Scott said. "What happened to 'don't talk to or about Ms. MacFarland that way'?"

Tommy turned his attention to Scott, and a frown darkened his brow. "Those instructions were specifically for you, Scott. And they still apply."

Scott sneered. "You really think you're better than me now, don't you? Got a little money, nicer clothes, a little attention from the ladies—"

"Fellas!" Jared said, wedging himself between the two of them. "Let's get this thing started. Hey, Rev!" He called over his shoulder. "Let's run everyone through this a time or two before it's time for dinner, huh?"

Pastor Evans shook his head at being called Rev but fell in step behind the wedding party to make his way to the side yard.

It was customary for the father of the groom to escort his wife to her seat before the ceremony. Tommy filled in for him, which wasn't uncustomary. The task filled him with delight that he didn't even bother to try to conceal.

When Brandi's father walked her down the aisle, that strange unnamable feeling I had earlier made my throat tight with emotion again. What was that? It wasn't sadness because I was truly happy for my son, but...it was something akin to that. Grief, maybe?

I cleared my throat and wiped away an errant tear. The motion drew Tommy's attention.

"You okay?" he mouthed.

I nodded and wiped away another tear, which didn't do much to convince him that I was. Disregarding my dismissal, he came over, handed me a real goddamn handkerchief, and sat next to me.

"Where do you even buy handkerchiefs anymore?" I asked with a wet laugh as I dabbed at the corners of my eyes.

"The same place you buy any sort of men's accessories. They aren't all that rare."

"And you just happen to have one on you right now?"

He shrugged, then took my hand in his. "I figured it would be handy for a situation such as this. I'm at your service, remember?"

I chuckled wetly. "Yeah, I remember."

His thumb stroked the center of my palm gently, and while the touch was still innocent, I felt it in not-so-innocent places.

"Tomás?" Pastor Evans called. "This is the part where you present the rings. It's a very important part of the ceremony. I've had best men miss their cue in the past—"

"I hear you, Rev," Tommy grumbled, giving my hand a squeeze, then went to stand next to Jared to hand over the rings.

"Man," James said, plopping gracelessly into the seat next to me. "What did you do to that boy to get him so sprung on you?"

"Sprung? On me? Nothing! And he's not sprung, so I don't know what you're talking about."

"Mmmhmm, like hell, you don't." James propped her feet up on the chair in front of her. "He's always had a thing for you, but I've been watching him watch you, and I can see that it's on a whole new level now. So, either you fucked him, or you're thinking about it. Which is it?"

"James!" I squawked then looked around frantically. Thankfully, most everyone had made their way back to the house to nibble on snacks in the kitchen and the bar, so no one overheard her. "He's Jared's best friend and young enough to be my son."

My sister's left eyebrow arrowed upward. "I notice that you didn't deny either of those things, either."

"There's nothing to deny, James. Nothing has happened!" I whispered a little too loudly.

James chuckled and turned toward me. "Darcy... Young boys like that are just toys. Something fun to play with. Not a thing to take seriously. As long as he understands that up-front, everyone gets what they need, everyone's happy, and no one gets hurt." She stood then, towering over me with her hands on her hips as if she'd said something wise and profound instead of provocative. "I'm gonna cut out early."

"You're not staying for the rehearsal dinner?" I asked.

Hands still on her hips, she looked around. "To be honest, this has been a lot of togetherness for me today," she said and didn't bother to explain herself any further. I understood, but I couldn't help feeling a little abandoned.

"Oh. Well, I guess I'll see y'all tomorrow afternoon," I said, standing to hug her.

James gave me a kiss on the cheek. "Okay, sis. And, hey..." She held me at arm's length so she could look me in the eyes. "If Tommy Martinez is down to do something strange with you while he's in town, let him."

"James—" I tried to push away from her completely, but she held me fast.

"Darcy, it's okay to take a little pleasure for yourself. You're overdue." She smacked another kiss on my cheek, chucked up the deuces, and said," See you later, nephew!" before exiting the rehearsal like everyone had convened to pay her tribute.

I watched James make her way across the lawn in her super skinny jeans, wild hair, and a cacophony of brass bangles. Not for the first time in my life, I wished I could be as loud, bold, and deficient of fucks as my sister. I've never been good at asking for or taking what I wanted.

When I turned toward the couple at the altar, stammering through their I dos, and I immediately felt Tommy's eyes on me. When I met his gaze, I couldn't help thinking that James wasn't wrong. I was overdue for some pleasure. Maybe it *was* time for me to take some for myself.

9

TOMÁS

Megan Thee Stallion and Cardi B's newest single blasted from the speakers of the private room I'd reserved for the bachelor party. I could tell by the big goofy-ass grin on Jared's face as two very talented dancers tag-teamed him in a very athletic, seemingly impossible twerk session that I'd done a good job. He'd asked for a drunken, debauched bachelor party, and if the sticky dollar-bill-littered floor and the empty bottles of liquor strewn about the room were any sort of measurement, both boxes had been checked. Not that I was worried.

I just wished I was having as much fun as everyone else.

The rehearsal dinner had dragged on, with me trying not to stare at Darcy all night. The bachelor party seemed intent on doing the same. Ordinarily, I would be all into a night spent with half-naked women bent on getting my dick hard, but now that I had *Darcy's To-Do List,* I couldn't think of anything else.

- *Kiss me. And I mean really kiss me. Not like you're just trying to get me naked, but like you could get lost in doing it for hours and hours. Stolen kisses. Secret kisses. Kisses in the rain. Kisses in the pool. Kiss me.*

- *Touch me. Trace my lips with the tips of your fingers. Learn the slope of my nose, the hollow of my throat, the curve of my breast with the tip of one finger. Trace each of those places again with the tip of your tongue.*

- *Talk to me. Tell me all the ways you imagined us together. Tell me every dirty thought you ever had. Every time a glancing touch made you hard — the way your hand cupping my shoulder made me wet today. Tell me every fantasy you ever had while laying in bed in the garçonnière. Tell me the meaning of all those Spanish pet names you've given me. Whisper them in my ear. Make me wet with your words.*

- *Make me come. You probably know lots of ways to make a woman come. I know you do. Show me.*

That last one...*shit*. That last one about did me in. I knew *sooo* many ways to make her come. I'd daydreamed about it *in fucking detail*. There was a catalog in my brain that I was ready to put to work. And now that I had this list, I would start to tick every single one of them off, one by one.

As soon as I got out of this fucking strip club.

The song ended, and the strippers climbed off of Jared, leaving him covered in glitter and looking deliriously happy. The DJ announced last call. That was my cue. These dudes were all drunk as hell, and I wanted to be out of the strip club before the lights came up.

"Hey, bruh," I said, tapping the bouncer standing by the door. "Can you let our waitress know that I'm ready to settle up?"

The big man gave me a short nod, opened the door, and

signaled for the waitress. I turned back to Jared, who was trying, unsuccessfully, to stand up.

"Hold on, Jay. I gotchu, man," I said, looping his arm over my shoulders to steady him.

"Wow. I'm a lot more drunk when I stand up."

"Heh, yeah. That happens," I said with a chuckle. "I think it's about time to pack it in for the night."

"Agreed," he said with an enthusiastic nod.

Arm in arm, we walked out to the curb just as our car was pulling up. When I climbed in and closed the door, Jared groaned. "You all right over there? You ain't gonna be sick, are you?"

"Nah... I was just thinking about sleeping in my old bedroom and realized that I'd much rather be sleeping next to Brandi tonight," my drunk friend admitted. He wasn't one to get all sappy about a girl, but this weekend was really bringing it out of him — which was appropriate, I guess.

"I mean, we could drop you off at her hotel instead. You could Romeo your way into her room."

"Pfft, I wish. She's so superstitious about not seeing each other before the wedding. There's no way she would let me in."

"Wow... By this time tomorrow, you'll be a married man."

"I know. Am I s'posed to feel nervous? 'Cause I don't. I'm just ready to start my life with her, you know?"

I shook my head. "I don't know, but I love that for you, man."

Jared chuckled dryly. "Yeah...you're right. You don't know," he said, then let the matter drop, but I heard something else in that dismissal that we should probably discuss at some point.

The house was quiet and dark when we pulled in. Assuming that Darcy had gone to bed, I made sure Jared made it to his third-floor bedroom safely and as quietly as possible. I'd avoided the dark plant-filled hallway on the way up, sticking to the piazza instead. Now I made my way to her bedroom door. It was closed, and there was no light under it, but I knocked anyway, hoping that she was still awake.

"Darcy?" I called softly, rapping my knuckles against the door again.

Nothing.

I allowed myself a sigh of disappointment and started toward the garçonnière. Did I really expect her to stay up until the wee hours of the morning to talk to me? Maybe I should just take this as a sign that I should let this go. Enjoy the weekend, celebrate my friend and his new bride, then carry my ass back to Chicago and get on with my life.

The predawn air was still humid and filled with night sounds — the meeps of little peeper tree frogs and the occasional rise and fall of a cicada whose own circadian rhythms were off. I checked to make sure the back door was locked before I headed toward the stairs up to the apartment, feeling a little wired and antsy. Midway up, I heard a loud splash. I paused and held my breath, and sure enough, I heard another one.

Darcy was in the pool.

Now locked out of the house, which was the easiest route to the pool, I hopped the fence into the yard, stumbled through some bushes, and crossed the grass until the pool was in full view.

Wearing a different swimsuit, this one black and covering far less skin than the one she had on yesterday, Darcy sliced through the brightly lit water almost soundlessly. I walked over to where I knew she would stop to flip around, took off my shoes, and dangled my feet in the water. Her form was perfect. She barely broke the surface to take in a breath before kicking her powerful legs to propel herself forward and knifing her hand through the water, so in the zone that when she came to the opposite end of the pool where I sat, she kicked me then star-tled, splashing to the surface.

"Oh, fuck!" she cursed. "How long have you been sitting there?"

"Long enough to see that you've become quite the athlete."

"Thank you," she answered shyly.

Fuck, she's beautiful. "Couldn't sleep?"

"I was waiting up for you," she said, her voice soft.

Nervous. *I'm fucking nervous, and she's looking at me like I have the answers.* "So, how about that drink?"

"Okay."

Planting her palms on the tiled patio, Darcy levered herself out of the pool. I stayed where I was and watched as each muscle in her lean arms engaged, and then her long legs until she was standing over me, water sluicing off her body, making her look like a mermaid out of a dark fairytale.

Sitting at her feet like this... Why did that make me hard almost instantly? *At your service...* Those words I'd tossed around playfully felt really fucking real right now.

I slipped my hand around her ankle and watched her skin pebble as I dragged my eyes over every inch of her until they met hers. She shivered a little, but I didn't think it was because she was cold.

She held out her hand. "You comin'?"

I was torn. I wanted to sit at her feet like this forever, but I also wanted to have the conversation that we'd been trying to have all day. Knowing where that conversation could lead, I took Darcy's proffered hand, and she led me inside.

The house was so quiet that it felt like someone had packed my ears with cotton. All of my senses were focused on Darcy. The sticky sound of her wet feet on the hardwood floors. The rustling leaves of the houseplants as our shoulders brushed against them in the closeness of the dark hallway. The way the door stuck and then jogged back when she twisted the knob, swollen and warped from years in the damp Charleston humidity. It was both real and unreal, yet I was in it, feeling every sensual detail.

"I'm just going to jump in the shower and rinse off the chlorine," she said, turning to me in the middle of the room. "But there's a little bar over there next to the piazza doors. Make yourself a drink, and I'll be right out."

While Darcy showered and put on another of her silky robes, I made both of us a drink. When she finished up in the shower, she joined me out on the piazza, and we sat on a patio set hidden behind a curtain of ivy. With the citronella candles lit and the pillows and cushions arranged just so, it was clear that she had set up this space for us to talk before I got here. The cozy seclusion enveloped us and sent a frisson of excitement across my skin. We'd sat out here together many a night. Back then, she would sit at the far end of the couch, as far away from me as she could be without sitting on another piece of furniture altogether. As the night progressed and the conversation became more intimate, she'd inch closer and closer until we were cuddled up at one end. Not tonight, though. Tonight, she sat right next to me. Close enough for me to see that her eyelashes were still wet and tangled. Close enough to smell her expensive perfumed soap mixed with the harsh chemical smell of chlorine.

"So, how did it go? Did you have any fun?"

"Not really. I was just a glorified chaperone with a Black Card. I barely drank tonight."

"Hm." She raised her glass to take a drink, and I did the same. I took a deep swallow that I hoped would calm, if not completely drown my nervousness.

"So, it's hard to know where to start," she said, twisting toward me on her cushion and tucking her feet under her. "I'm still very much thinking and feeling the same way I felt this morning when we had our talk on the back porch. And sitting here next to you tonight, I just keep thinking... 'This is Tommy. You can't do this with Tommy.'"

What was this feeling? Disappointment? I brought my glass to my lips once more to hide whatever the feeling was.

"But then I remembered this afternoon in my study. The way you were with me, and how it felt to hold your hand and that almost kiss last night. Just our lips brushing together. It was more intense than any real kiss I've had in years, and...I don't know, Tommy. I don't know if I can do this... I just... I think..."

"You just think what, Darcy?" I asked softly. "Do you think you need a little push?"

"Yeah?" she said with a shrug.

I laughed and shook my head. "That sounded a little bit like a question and not an answer."

"And you sound a little mean," she said with narrowed eyes. "And shouldn't it be a question? This is not who I am. I'm a good woman—"

"Good to who, Darcy? From where I'm sitting, you're good to everyone but you."

She recoiled a little. "You don't know what you're talking about."

"I don't?" Now would be a good time to shut up. I was probably in danger of saying too much, but she said she wanted a push, so I'd give it to her. "Maybe you're so used to hearing lies that the truth sounds foreign to you."

"And what's the truth?" she asked.

"The truth is that you're a good woman who settled for a shallow puddle of a man and then wondered why you found no depth there. You're a good woman who isn't good to herself. Or to know when or how to grab something good when it's being offered."

"And you think that good thing is you?" she asked with a raised brow.

I shook my head. "I don't know, Darcy. I know that I want you, but you have to make that decision for yourself. Which was part of the reason why I asked you to make that list."

"You and this list," she groaned. "A list of the ways I want and need to be pleased by you doesn't change the circumstances. I'm not that woman, Tommy. I'm not some desperate—"

"No. Don't do that," I warned, pointing at her. "Don't form your pretty mouth to make yourself sound like some lonely, desperate woman who's being coerced into this. It's an insult to both of us. And let's be real, it's not true. You don't need to be this tightly-strung ball of want and need. You know you could have any man you want."

"But that's the problem, isn't it? I don't want just any man, Tommy," she said. Her voice had gone soft, somewhere between a rasp and a whisper, and she was wearing that look again. That look that said she wanted me to kiss her. We stared at each other for a few long moments, but neither of us made a move.

"Darcy... If you want me, you're going to have to—"

She reached for me. Grabbed a fistful of my shirt, hauled me closer. "I'm going to have to what?" she whispered hotly. "Do this?"

I barely had a chance to nod before she gave me an eager, searching kiss.

I dreamed of this so many times. Ran through this first kiss so many times in my mind that I thought I would know exactly what to do when it finally happened. I'd imagined that she would be frantic like this and that I would know exactly how to slow it down. But I've wanted her for so long that I didn't... I couldn't... Slowing down wasn't an option. I just let her take. When she reached for me, when she slanted her mouth over mine, parted her lips, and slid inside, I let her. I let her take what she needed.

In one quick movement, she maneuvered herself into my lap, pressing her body right up against mine. The moan that rumbled up from my chest when she ground her pussy against my already hard dick probably echoed through every empty room in the house. I was trying to be sweet and easy, but what I wanted from this kiss had become ungentlemanly very quickly. I thrust my tongue in the sweet place behind her lips, mouth-fucking her until her whimpers and sighs poured out like water. Darcy returned my kisses with a recklessness that all but accused me of waking up the little beast inside her. Made it bare its teeth. Made her want to devour me. And fuck, if this was how it felt to be eaten alive, I couldn't think of a better way to die.

Her body burned under the thin layers of silk that slipped and slid over her skin as I gripped her waist, barely holding on as her hips made impatient circles in my lap, grinding her pussy against my dick so perfectly that I couldn't help moaning. There were no shouldn'ts or mustn'ts in the way she rubbed her pussy against me, damn near forcing me to play counterpoint. I shifted my hands from her waist to grip her hips, lifting mine so that the next roll of her hips met the split of her pussy lips and made her breath catch.

She cursed softly and bunched the shoulders of my shirt in her hands.

God... I wanted to strip her naked and give her what her body was asking for, but I needed her to take the initiative. It would be so easy for me to give her another little push. To flip her onto her back on this heirloom wicker furniture, strip off every layer of the expensive silk on her body, and fuck her. But in the morning, it would be too easy for her to dismiss what happened. Too easy for her to say she got caught up in the moment, and it couldn't happen again.

I shook my head and laughed. "The way you're moving, and all of these little sounds that you're making..." I cupped her face in both my hands and nipped at her lips. "You're gonna make me come in my pants if you keep it up."

Her hips rotated in a tight little circle, and I swear I felt her pussy pulse and tighten, but it had to be impossible to feel that through all these layers of clothes, right?

She smiled against my mouth. "Same. I'm so wet and so close that if you touched me right now..."

My dick thumped hard, spilling a bit of precum near my hip at hearing those words. "Is that what you want, Darcy? Tell me you want me to—"

"Touch me. Touch my pussy," she whispered, her face buried in my neck.

Sliding one hand down between our bodies and pushing her loose silk shorts aside, I trailed my fingers through the pulsing, wet space between her thighs. "Fuck, hermosa...you weren't kidding. You're drenched," I mumbled, nibbling at her shoulder and the side of her neck. She was trembling now and pressing her pussy into my palm, wanting more. "You just want me to touch it?" I asked, trailing my fingertips up and down the delicate furls of her outer lips.

"No..."

"What do you need, pretty baby? You want to ride my hand? You want me to see how many of my fingers your needy pussy can take?" *Needy.* I had some nerve calling her needy when all I could think about was how much I needed to be slamming my dick into her needy little pussy. I licked a path along the line of her neck, nibbled on her earlobe. "You need me to play with your clit?" I pinched it between my thumb and the knuckle of my forefinger.

"Tommy!" she gasped, more of her silky wetness spilling over my fingers.

"Tell me what you want me to do. Do you want me to make you come, Darcy?"

"Yes! Make me come," she panted against my lips, a desperate sound.

"Fuck, yes," I whispered back, plunging my middle two fingers into her. Tight, satiny, and so, so, wet. Her hips snapped forward, sinking my fingers deeper. I cradled her in my hand, stroking them deep and feeling her tighten around them. She rubbed her clit against the heel of my hand, needing that extra bit of stimulation, but when I added a third finger, she went completely still.

"Shit, Tommy," she whispered, then arched and threw her head back.

"Hermosa, coño...e' perfecto," I whispered, my hand still in her pussy, feeling it flex around my fingers in hard spasms — close to coming. Almost, but not yet. She looked at me, her still wet hair tangled around her shoulders, her swim-hard body strong and undulating as waves of pleasure coursed through her. I've wanted to have her like this — wanted her to want this from me. Wanted that wild look in her eyes as I pressed my thumb to her clit and the swollen, rough bundle of nerves against the front wall of her pussy and rubbed those fingers inside and outside of her like I was testing and observing the subtle changes in her texture and wetness (because I was) until she trembled and moaned.

I want to see her come, I want to see her come, I need to see it...

I wanted to see how she looked when she came apart from my attentions. Wanted my name in her mouth when she came. Needed it. But...*fuck.*

I never considered what would happen to me. Never considered how I would feel if she said yes, and then *Tommy!* and yes and yes again. I never considered what would happen to me or how the fuck it would make me feel.

My body suddenly felt too light to stay tethered to earth. Like if she wasn't on top of me, I would've careened into the black velvet night sky. As she curled over me, panting her ecstasy into my mouth between fierce, untamed kisses, I followed her right over the cliff, coming so hard that I felt the actual sensation of falling, a weightlessness that sparked an adrenaline-laced spike of pleasure that made me cling to her. I crushed her to me with one hand while the other was still inside of her.

"Oh, Tommy..." she whispered, tears in her voice as another orgasm ripped through her, making her pussy spasm so hard that it pushed my fingers out of her. I covered her pussy with the flat of my palm, not inside of her anymore but wanting to feel every twitch and throb it made as she came from the pleasure I gave her. Gradually, I settled back into my skin, pleasure still crackling and popping along my nerve endings, but now that the world had swung back into focus, I felt drugged. My limbs felt weighted down from my release. Darcy was in my arms, warm, sticky with sweat and cum, and humming contentedly. I buried my face in her hair and breathed her in.

Hmmm... This is dangerous, but I'm going to enjoy every minute of it.

"Come on," I murmured, rocking forward and shifting her in my arms so that I could support her weight. "Let's get you to bed."

Darcy wrapped her legs and arms around me and kissed me as I walked through the room, now only semi-dark with pale dawn light. At the edge of the bed, she shrugged out of her robe and let it fall to the floor. I pulled back the coverlet and laid her down in the cool, white sheets. The moment I set her down, she stripped off the thin-strapped silk chemise and flirty sleep shorts unceremoniously, revealing her body to me, and for a moment... I couldn't fucking breathe. Her breasts were small, but her dark berry nipples made me want them in my mouth. My palms itched to caress every inch of her soft skin, and play between her legs again. She wasn't bare, but the hair there was soft and neatly trimmed. I was glad to have the answer to that question now. With a sly smile on her lips, she burrowed into the white sheets.

"Come here..." she whispered. "Take your clothes off, and get in here with me." She stretched out her arm, palm upward, beckoning.

"Darcy... You're killing me. You know I can't. It's already dawn."

"Jared won't be up for another couple of hours. We can cuddle until then—"

"If by cuddle, you mean cuddling my dick into your wet, tight pussy, I'm absolutely sure I should not get into this bed." The words were out before I could rein them in. It was so vulgar. I tried not to talk to her that, but well, shit. That was exactly what I wanted to do, so why pretend?

Darcy chuckled softly, and her hand remained outstretched. Her long, slim, brown fingers slightly curled, beckoning me into her bed, and *fuck*... I wanted to go to her. I wanted to go to her and kiss her and cuddle-fuck her until we were both so deliriously tired that we'd sleep for a week.

"Tomorrow's Jared's wedding," I said finally. "And as much as I want to be with you tonight, I don't want to do anything that might ruin—"

"You're right," she whispered with a sigh. "Goodnight, Tommy."

I leaned across the bed and gave her one last kiss. "Goodnight, Darcy."

10

DARCY

When I woke up in the morning, my hand was already on my pussy. I couldn't remember the last time that happened, or if it ever had happened before. Not even on the morning of my own wedding. But here I was, rolling over onto my back with my hand between my legs.

Things with Tommy had swung from barely acknowledged attraction to us devouring each other unchecked. What made me cross the line and land right in his lap, I couldn't be sure. But he rewarded my boldness with that kiss.

Maybe what my sister said about taking some pleasure for myself and what Tommy said about me never being good to myself just made me realize that yes, I wanted this — wanted him — and a good woman would take the pleasure he offered.

So, I said yes.

And damn... I thought I knew how it felt to be desired until I said yes. I thought I understood how it felt to be on the receiving end of a man's desires, but not this man. Most men are initiators, takers...not Tommy. He let me take from him — and feeling that power seesaw in my direction made me unsteady, at first, and more than a little unsure. But then he whispered, "Tell me what you want me to do. Do you want me to make you come, Darcy?" And when I said yes, he pushed my panties to the side and did exactly that.

Remembering the desperate sounds I made in that moment made my cheeks flush hot, but the memory of how he'd reacted to my answer made my fingers slip into my already wet pussy. The look in his eyes and the things he whispered to me... It felt like reverence and sounded like prayers.

Now that I knew how it felt to have his hands on me, my own weren't enough. Frustrated, I reached for my phone, intending to tell him how I wasn't satisfied with my own hand after he touched me, only to find a message waiting.

TOMMY: *are you playing with your pussy right now, hermosa?*

I laughed out loud, but that laugh became a moan when the next message came through.

TOMMY: *cause I woke up thinking about you coming in my lap and now my hand is on my dick*

ME: *let me see*

A few moments passed before a short video came through. The still was of his hand mid-stroke on that beautiful dick I'd watched him play with in the shower yesterday morning. *Jesus Christ...* It was still hard to believe that he was carrying all of that around in his pants this whole time. Hiding that in those little soccer shorts and the skinny jeans they all wore.

I hit play.

"Hmm..." he moaned as his hand executed a slow tug at his

long, thick length. "Good morning, Darcy," he whispered, his voice raspy and playful.

Wow...Am I really sexting with Tommy? I shouldn't be okay with this. It should make me uncomfortable, but...damn...it didn't. Not even a little bit. All it made me feel was wetter.

I thumbed up my video app one-handed and pushed the blankets off my naked body with the other.

I pushed record.

"Good morning, Tommy," I murmured, stroking my fingers through my slippery folds and then holding them up so that he could see how wet I was. Before I could second-guess myself, I sent the video.

Hand still on my pussy, I waited for the video to send and deliver. A few seconds passed, then an ellipsis appeared.

TOMMY: *damn, flaca.*
Dywmtcoaeyptycomf?

I frowned at that last jumble of letters. Was he jerking off with his other hand and thumbed that out by accident?

ME: *what was that alphabet soup?*
Are you okay or are you
having a seizure over there?

TOMMY: *it's an acronym.*
Do You Want Me To Come
Over And Eat Your Pussy
'Til You Come On My Face?

"Oh my god!" I gasped aloud while thumbing out *yes!* with more than one exclamation point. But just as the message sent, a scheduled alert appeared on my phone, and after yesterday, I knew it came up on his phone at the same time.

caterers arrive in 45 min

"Shit," I cursed with a frustrated groan.

ME: coffee?

TOMMY: meet you in the kitchen in five
I have some business I need to handle first
Thank you for the video
It'll make it easier to handle that business

THAT BUSINESS... I knew exactly how he handled that business. I'd witnessed it with my own eyes. And honestly... I was pissed I couldn't see it right now.

ME: record it for me?

TOMMY: okay, hermosa.
anything you want.

Anything you want... Those fucking words were going to be my ruination. I felt it in my bones.

I threw my phone aside because if I waited for and watched that video, my sister would find me in the bed with my hand between my legs. Plus, I wanted to meet him in the kitchen for coffee. To grab a private moment before the day began and the wedding festivities kicked into high gear.

I washed my face, brushed my teeth, finger-combed my sleep-tangled hair into a silk turban, pulled on the ground-skimming robe that matched, knotted it at the waist, and made my way downstairs.

Murmuring a bright greeting to my beautiful monstera, I glided into the foyer where the door stood propped open for the catering company to bring tables in. Glancing to the left, I saw that the living room had been cleared of furniture, and bar-height tables skirted the designated dance floor. A little further down the hall, men were clearing out the furniture in the formal dining room.

"Good morning, fellas!" I called out, clutching at my robe as a breeze off the river tunneled through the open doors. "Everything okay?"

"Yes, ma'am!" one of the men said in response. "We've got everything handled."

"All right, then. If you want anything to drink — coffee, juice, water — just let me or Minnie know."

"Thank you, ma'am."

So much for a quiet, private moment before the day began. This wedding was already happening. My son was getting married — in this house where I'd raised him. And all I could think about was his best friend Tommy and wonder if he came for me yet. *What the fuck did that make me?*

The main hallway was packed with men at work, so I took the back one that led to the laundry room and a little powder room. Minnie was probably in the kitchen already, and I just wanted to hold onto this feeling for a moment longer. This feeling of just being Darcy — a whole and sexual woman, not just someone's mother and ex-wife. I wanted to float on this feeling until I saw Tommy and shared a cup of coffee with him on the back porch.

Just as I approached the laundry room, a hand shot out, hooked around my waist, and hauled me inside. I barely had a moment to gasp or protest before Tommy pressed my back against the pocket door, locked it, and kissed me.

His kiss, his kiss, his goddamn kiss... It was like an accelerant for the demands that my body, mind, and pussy had made for years. Demands that went unanswered until he ignited them — ignited *me*. With one stroke of his tongue, my body arched into him. I grabbed his waist and pulled him right up against me.

"I've got something for you," he whispered against my lips.

"What?"

He was in pajama bottoms and a t-shirt and looked every bit the college boy that lived in the apartment over my garage for a year. Still sweet and attentive, but broader, and sexier, and dirtier...definitely dirtier as he'd pulled out a pair of AirPods and his phone with a video queued up on the screen.

"Wait..." He turned and looked at the dryer. "How do you turn this thing on? Do you have something we can put in here that's kinda loud?"

"Why?"

"You don't want anyone to hear us in here, do you?" he asked, his voice low and suggestive and a mischievous look in his eye.

I grabbed two of the big dryer balls, threw them in the front loader, and selected the quick cycle.

"Yeah, that'll work," he said with a nod, then bullied me up against the door again.

"What do you have for me?"

"Your video... I was going to send it to you, but I kinda figured you wouldn't take time to watch it before you came down, so..." He put the phone in my hand and the AirBuds in my ears. "But first...can I see your wet pussy again?"

"Yes," I whispered, looking directly in his eyes as I parted my robe and watching as he looked down to where I was bare underneath the silk.

Tommy let out a long, deep moan. "I remember the first time I saw you in one of these robes. It was in the kitchen, and you were making me lemon ricotta pancakes before I went to class. I always wondered if you were naked under them. I'm glad to know that my fantasy isn't just a fantasy... Show me, Darcy. Let me see how wet you are," he whispered, his voice hoarse with need.

That little glimpse into his memory. Me in the kitchen, making him breakfast, and him fantasizing about me... It made this moment feel even dirtier.

I pushed two fingers inside, barely able to hold back my moans.

"Fuck..." he cursed softly when I showed him the slippery evidence of what he'd asked for. "Still so, so wet," he whispered. "You didn't even take care of yourself, did you?" he asked.

"I—"

"I know you didn't," he interrupted, sinking down to his knees. "You prettied yourself up and rushed down here to meet me for coffee. You neglected your pussy."

"There wasn't time. I wanted—"

"You gotta learn to put your oxygen mask on first, Darcy."

"That's not what that mea—" But my retort was cut short by his warm tongue dragging over my sensitive pussy.

He pursed his lips and placed a delicate kiss right above my clit. Looking up at me, he bracketed my hips with his hands. "Let me take care of you, Darcy," he whispered, his thumbs stroking comforting circles on the jut of my hip bones.

"But people are out there setting up for the wedding. My sister and the rest of the bridesmaids will be here soon, and—"

"All of that can wait. The wedding will still happen if you aren't there to greet them the second they walk in. Minerva is out there. She can handle things while I take care of you."

"I... This is Jared and Brandi's day. I want everything to be perfect for them."

"And it will be...even if you pause for ten minutes to let me eat your pussy."

"Tommy..." My cheeks flushed so hot that I had to cover them with my palms. "We can't. I shouldn't," I repeated.

"Darcy... Darcy, look at me," he demanded.

Swallowing down my embarrassment, I dropped my hands to my sides and looked down at him.

"Spread your legs so I can take care of you. Please," he added, punctuating his request with a devilish smirk.

My fucking god. Like I could deny his request. No woman on this earth could say no to that.

I pressed my upper back to the door and spread my legs for him. Tommy let out a sweet sigh, and his warm breath buffeted my wet pussy, cooling my heated skin. He slid his hand up my inner thigh and spread me even wider.

"Yes, pretty baby. Just like that," he whispered, then drew his nose along the crease of my inner thigh, scenting me.

A loud thunk sounded somewhere on the main floor, and I tensed, wondering what had been dropped or knocked over, but then Tommy split my pussy lips with his tongue, and the only thing that mattered was what he was doing between my thighs.

"Christ, you taste so fucking good. Damn, I wish I could take my time with you, but we have a schedule to keep. Play the video, hermosa. And turn the volume up."

The phone. I'd forgotten it was in my hand the moment he put his mouth on me. I raised it up to eye level and pressed play. Turned the volume up.

He was standing in the bathroom, holding the phone up to the mirror. His shirt was still on but pushed up over his head, and his pajama bottoms, the same ones he had on now, were pushed down just enough for his hand to plunge inside and pull out his dick. It appeared like some sort of magic trick. Safely tucked away, and then hello, massive, lovely penis! I'd seen it before, but I was still surprised by it.

Moans, Tommy's moans, filled my ears as the screen displayed a video of him, standing opposite the mirror, strong, proud, young, and so fucking gorgeous with one hand caressing his hardness.

"This is yours, Darcy. For as long as you want it," he whispered on the video.

Tommy gripped my hip firmly and covered my pussy with his mouth as the noise-canceling earbuds in my ears dampened the sounds of the men in my house moving tables and the clinks of glass and dinnerware and replaced them with Tommy's soft, low voice, whispering in Spanish as he drizzled bath oil onto his dick.

"¿Ves? Ves lo que me haces? So hard for you, Darcy. This is what you do to me."

Every single one of my senses was on overload. I watched as he made himself slick and shiny with that bath oil I left in the shower for guests. It was Neutrogena. Hypoallergenic. Cheap, but you could trick folks into thinking it was fancy if you put it in a nice bottle. I knew the exact smell of that body oil. I could smell it on him now. I wanted to yank his pajama bottoms down and bury my nose between his legs so that I could smell him and that clean scent. To know how it smelled on his skin. Know what scents filled the room when Tommy fucked his dick into his fist.

Gripping my hip in one hand, Tommy gave me one broad, thorough lick as he slid two of his thick fingers inside of me. At least, I thought it was two. I couldn't be sure because my attention was split between the Tommy at my feet and the Tommy making needy moans in my ears and desperately fucking his hand on-screen.

He focused his attention on my clit, his tongue applying just the right amount of pressure before licking and suckling at the hard nub. It was a sensory deprivation exercise designed to make me come.

"Mmm," I moaned, tipping my hips forward a little more so his fingers could reach a little deeper, and my sex could fit more flush against his mouth, sealing the now puffy lips and my hard clit in that decadent heat. His clever tongue swept and swirled over my clit; his fingers were impossibly deep.

"It took everything in me not to crawl into bed with you last night. Eat your pussy until you begged me to fuck you. To feel you clench and gush all over me every time I push in and out of you. In and out...in and out until my dick's slick and wet from being inside you. Fuck... I almost climbed in that bed, Darcy. I almost climbed in that bed and fucked you." Video Tommy whispered those last two words, spilling precum on his fingers.

My pussy clenched in response, and Tommy twisted his fingers inside of me, making me moan so loud that I was sure if there was anyone in the hall or the kitchen, they surely heard me.

I didn't care.

He whispered something against my pussy. Something I couldn't hear, but I felt his lips shape around the words between licks of my clit. I grabbed a fistful of his hair, and he moaned. I didn't hear that either, but it reverberated through me. God, the way he sucked on my clit was perfect, so perfect that my pussy clenched and fluttered around his fingers, my pleasure a promise that he was determined to deliver.

"I wanted it so badly..." video Tommy continued. "I wanted to bury my dick so deep inside of you that when you came again, I'd feel it from the tip of my dick to the base. Then fuck you slow and deep until you came again. You hear me, pretty baby?"

"Yes," I breathed in response to video Tommy's question and

what real-life Tommy was doing down on his knees between my thighs.

Video Tommy moaned. "What would you sound like? Would you make those same kitty growls? Or would you get loud for me? Or maybe you would smother your moans and screams into my shoulder? Maybe you'd bite my shoulder because I felt so damn good to you? Bite and lick and then bite me again while your pussy clenched and soaked my dick the way you soaked my lap last night." His breath hitched and shuddered in my ears. My breathing mirrored his, and I watched wide-eyed as video Tommy fucked his fist, and real-life Tommy spun me up with his mouth and fingers.

I bit my bottom lip hard, trying not to scream...but fuck, it felt good. So, so good. "Tommy," I gasped hoarsely because I was close.

When video Tommy came, the sound of his satisfied moans filled my ears, and I moaned and came along with him while real-life Tommy drank me up like he was oh so thirsty.

The video ended, and my head and ears filled with the raspy sounds of my own breath soughing in and out of my lungs, barely covered by the bump and tumble of the dryer balls as they finished up the quick cycle.

Tommy planted wet kisses on my thighs, my lower belly, and my hips. His fingers — gentler now, but still inside of me — created delicious waves of pleasure. He stood slowly, slipped his fingers out of me just as slowly, and wiped his chin with the back of his hand with a big grin on his face. My vision was hazy, soft around the edges in a way that made his beautiful, messy face look like something out of a dream sequence in a John Hughes movie.

He took the AirPods out of my ears and his phone out of my hand, then tucked both into the pocket of his pajama bottoms.

Still smiling at me, he leaned in and placed a soft kiss on my lips. "Look at you," he whispered.

I blinked and slid my hands around his waist. "What? What do I look like?"

"Softer and more relaxed than I've ever seen you," he whispered, brushing a loose curl away from my face. "Sated but still wanting more, like a kid staring at the dessert table. Wait...maybe I'm talking about myself," he said with a laugh, but it died on his tongue when he glanced downward, his eyes devouring my still exposed skin. "Am I right? Do you want more?"

He traced the tip of his finger between my breasts, down the center of me, stopping short of my mound. My hips tipped forward of their own volition.

"Yes," I whispered.

Tommy grunted a noncommittal sound of agreement then closed my robe. Holding the lapels firmly to conceal my nakedness, he brushed his lips against my neck, my cheek, and my lips, where he lingered to nibble and lick. I tasted myself on his mouth, and it made me want him between my legs again. And his dick... I wanted the dick he said was mine, too.

For as long as you want it...

The dryer stopped, and the sounds it had dampened from the other side of the door filtered in. He moaned against my mouth again, but it was a frustrated sound.

"Más, más, más," he whispered then pulled away slowly. "Nunca lo suficiente para mi."

I frowned and shook my head. "All I understood was more, more, more."

He chuckled softly. "That's all you really need to understand."

But whatever else he'd said had sounded sorrowful, and he was trying to make light of it now.

"Tommy—"

"Count to fifty, then meet me in the kitchen, okay?"

I nodded. "Okay."

He reached behind me and flicked the lock on the pocket door. "Oh, and there's a new appointment on our shared calendar."

"What for?" I asked, stepping out of the way of the door.

Tommy's lips quirked, and he gave me a wink. "You'll see," he said, then closed the pocket door between us.

Still struggling to steady myself, I pressed my forehead to the door. My body was still tingling and thrumming from the orgasm he gave me, but I still wanted to yank it open and pull him back in.

"Count, Darcy," he said from the other side.

I laughed and took a deep breath. "One, two, three, four..."

By the time I'd counted to fifty, my heart rate had slowed to a regular pace, but my body had slipped into the languid state that followed a deeply satisfying orgasm. I'd much rather be rolling over to stretch myself over and along Tommy's naked body, but instead, I shuffled into the kitchen.

"Good morning, Darcy," Minerva said cheerily, but then she gave me a look. A look that said that she might have heard Tommy break his fast by eating my pussy and me moaning loud enough to drown out the dryer balls bouncing around on the quick cycle.

"Morning, Minnie," I said, feeling my neck, face, and ears flush hot with embarrassment.

"Coffee?"

"Yeah, I'll take a cup."

"You look a little flushed," she said with a note of faux concern in her voice, then smirked.

Yeah...she heard us. If I was reading her right, she didn't disapprove.

"Good morning, Darcy," Tommy said, his voice soft, but the baritone depth of it resonated in the room and in my still throbbing pussy.

"Morning, Tommy," I answered back, barely able to get my voice above a heated whisper. "How'd you sleep?" I asked after clearing my throat.

"Good, which is surprising, considering how late we were out—"

"How late were we out?" Jared grumbled, shuffling into the kitchen. "And why'd you let me drink so damn much?"

"Let you?" Tommy retorted, bringing his coffee cup to his lips. Those lips that were so good at kissing mine — both sets of them.

Jesus... My mind will not get out of the fucking gutter.

"Yeah, let me," Jared said again while pulling me in to kiss me on the forehead. I stiffened for a moment, worried that he might smell Tommy on me, but realized after catching a whiff of him that he couldn't smell a thing over the fermented stench seeping out of his pores.

"Good lord, boy! You smell like you bathed in a bottle of Marrow Bone Creek!" I exclaimed, pushing him away.

"See, Tommy! You let me drink too much!"

"Once again, *let you?* Last time I checked, you were a grown-ass man who knew his own limits. I was only responsible for getting you to and from the strip club without incident. Which I did."

The boys went back and forth like that. Playful bickering that again made me remember other mornings when they had elbowed each other through a meal and horsed around. I used to love the racket they made. When they were away, the house was too quiet.

"All right, you two," Minerva said when they started to get

too carried away. She put two plates full of breakfast fare in front of them, and they settled, elbows out, and started to eat.

Tommy looked up at me in the midst of forking a mouthful of grits and eggs in his mouth. His mood may have been playful, but his eyes were anything but. They were molten pools of want that made my nipples peak against my silk robe.

"So, what's the schedule look like today?" Jared asked.

"Nothing until we head over to the barbershop this afternoon."

"Good," I interjected. "That gives you time to get a workout in. Sweat that liquor out of your system." As I brought the coffee cup to my lips, I thought of Tommy shirtless and running along Battery Park the way he often did when he lived here. How hadn't I noticed how fit he was then? Was it just mom-brain blocking all of that out? Because god... I couldn't stop thinking of him that way now. Shouldn't I feel ashamed? Guilty? Both?

When our eyes met again, all I felt was hungry, naked want.

Clattering heels sounded in the front hallway, and my sister James barreled into the kitchen. "Sorry I'm late, Darcy! I couldn't find my good flat iron, and the store was out of the dye I usually use on your hair, so I'll have to mix it— oh! Good morning, boys!" She painted on a smile, a sultry one that made Tommy sit up and pay attention.

I clenched my teeth.

"Good morning, Auntie," Tommy said with a big grin.

James all but growled at that greeting, but I don't think Tommy would label hers as the kitten type.

"I'm not your fucking Auntie, Tomás," she said, ruffling the hair I had just dug my fingers in as I came. "You really didn't bring a date to this thing?"

He raised a brow then glanced at me.

"Oh," she said with a snort. "That Mother of the Groom Concierge thing... You're not serious about that, are you?"

Tommy chuckled, then leaned in and gave her a kiss on the cheek. "Of course, I am. But I'll save you a dance, huh?" he promised with a wink. Then he turned and thumped Jared on the back. "I'm gonna change into some shit to work out in. Come get me when you're ready."

Jared nodded, still shoveling food into his face. I watched surreptitiously as Tommy left the kitchen and walked up the back path to the garçonnière.

"Auntie, can you not flirt with Tomás? It kinda creeps me out."

James rolled her eyes and turned to me. "Where are we gonna do this? Upstairs in your bathroom?"

I nodded, took some of the gear she'd dragged in, and helped her carry it up the stairs.

"That boy has got it bad for you, Darcy," she said, dropping her gear on my now freshly-made bed. Minerva must have snuck up here to make it while we were in the kitchen. I had a momentary vision of her checking the sheets like one of Queen Elizabeth's ladies-in-waiting.

We must know her proper functions...

The thought made me giggle, and James must have misinterpreted my giggling as a response to what she'd said.

"I'm serious, Darcy! That boy looks at you like he wants to slurp you up like an oyster."

"Ew, James! Why you gotta be so vulgar?" I asked, searching for my phone. Finding it on the night table nearest the French doors, I grabbed it and opened the messaging app. There were several messages waiting to be read, but I only cared about one.

"I'm just saying. You should really do something about that. Seriously."

"Do something about it?"

"Yes, do something about it. Say yes to him, or cut him loose so someone else can have a go."

"I have no idea what you're even talking about," I murmured, a slow smile spreading across my face when I saw what he had scheduled for us.

dick appt @ 12 a.m. EST

Oh, my god. I pressed a hand to my lower belly as I selected *yes* with my thumb.

11

TOMÁS

My knees were complaining by the time Jared and I reached the far end of Battery Park. It was a bit late in the afternoon for this. The sun was nearly at its peak, and the humidity was so thick that it made it difficult to breathe. The afternoon breeze coming off the river offered little relief. Those conditions made this run exactly what it was intended to be: cleansing. And if I were to judge by the stench rolling off of Jared, it seemed to be exactly that. I'd hoped it would cleanse me of some of the foolish thoughts circling in my head.

Thoughts about Darcy. Thoughts about us together.

Nunca lo suficiente para mi.

That realization had never been more clear than it became when I was down on my knees in that laundry room with Darcy. With the folds of her pussy glistening, begging for my mouth and fingers, my name on her lips, her voice soft and lost, and my heart pounding in my chest, I realized it then. I knew, I knew, *I fucking knew* that it was never going to be enough for me.

When I licked my lips, I could still taste her — earthy and sweet. A taste that I'd probably chase forever. Maybe the rest of my life. When I stretched my fingers, I thought of the silken clutch of her pussy, and the rough bundle of nerves just inside of her that made her hips pitch, roll, and buck against my mouth. When I closed my eyes, I saw her, robe gaping, breasts bared, eyes narrowed to glazed slits as she came.

I did that to her. I gave her that pleasure.

And tonight, I would have her again. Her panting, ragged breaths, and the way she growled into my mouth. I would get the chance to make her come with more than just my fingers and my tongue. *Tonight...* I would have that tonight. But damn it... It would never, never, never be enough for me.

"Shit!" Jared cursed loudly, his voice penetrating the music blaring from my AirPods. I slowed and turned, just in time to see him stumble on weak legs toward a nearby trashcan and throw up his breakfast.

Laughing, I pulled my phone out, turned off my music, and walked toward him. I'd set a punishing pace for our run because I was trying to put some distance between me and my thoughts, but apparently, it served a dual purpose — purging Jared of all the liquor he drank last night.

"Aw, champ... Do you feel better now?" I asked, giving him a couple of thumps on the back.

"Fuck you," he gurgled, then pulled off his shirt to wipe his face and mouth. "And actually, yes. I do feel better."

"Good, you wanna keep running, or—"

"Nah, let's just walk. I don't think there's anything left in there, but I'd rather not throw up in a public trashcan again."

"Fair enough."

Shoulder to shoulder, we fell in step, moving toward the right side of the sidewalk to make room for the other people who were foolish enough to go running at this time of day. Now that we weren't running, I'd started to sweat, my body trying desperately to cool me down. I pulled off my own shirt and mopped the sweat from my face. My phone chimed in my pocket. I pulled it out and checked my notifications, biting back a smile when I saw that Darcy had accepted my dick appointment invite.

"What's up? We got somewhere to be?" Jared asked.

"Just a reminder for the barbershop appointment. We have an hour," I lied, shoving the phone back into my pocket. Surprisingly, I was looking forward to our appointment at the high-end shop — a hot shave, a shoulder, neck, and scalp massage, and a haircut. It would feel good to be pampered after this run.

But not more than I was looking forward to that dick appointment with Darcy.

"So, that thing with my Aunt James this morning? What was that about?"

I frowned and gave him a sideways glance. "What thing with your Aunt James? What are you talking about?"

"The kiss on the cheek, and all that 'saving a dance for her' business. Are you trying to push up on my Auntie for real?"

I shook my head and laughed. James? That was who he was worried about? I'd flirted with Darcy in his presence every moment since we arrived, and he was worried about his wild-ass Auntie James?

"I'm just saying," he continued. "Me and Auntie James are close. It would be weird if y'all...got involved."

Sobering at his serious tone, I gave him a reassuring tap on the shoulder. "Relax, Jay. I'm not trying to get with your Auntie like that."

"Seriously, Tomás. Don't fuck my Auntie."

"Seriously, Jay. I won't fuck your Auntie."

But I'm absolutely going to fuck your mother.

———

A FEW HOURS LATER, with a fresh cut, a crisp tux, and the sun sinking in the sky, kissing the horizon with pink, orange, and purple hues, Jared was ready to meet Brandi at the end of the aisle and say his I dos. At least, he was physically ready. The nerves that he had managed to keep at bay for months now showed up in full force.

"She's too good for me, bro," he muttered, pacing the living room of the garçonnière. "You've known me my whole adult life. You know I ain't shit. But Brandi... She's smart and ambitious. She's a fucking neurosurgeon, for fuck's sake. A fucking genius." He shook his head. "She deserves better. She could do so much better than me."

Not usually the type of dude given to talking about his insecurities or shortcomings, it was a bit unnerving to hear Jared doubt whether he was the right man for Brandi. I had no idea that he'd ever been intimidated by her intelligence or ambition. In fact, he always seemed to be in awe of her. And having witnessed their relationship from the sidelines, I knew that Brandi truly loved him.

"What are you even talking about, Jay? Yeah, she could've done better, but she chose your ass anyway."

"Fuck you—"

"I mean, do you seriously think she woke up this morning and suddenly realized your lack of depth? You've been together for three years. I assure you, she is aware."

We both knew that wasn't true. Jared was far from ignorant — shallow, yes, but there was no way that Brandi had ever questioned his intelligence. They were both surgeons, both ambitious, and complemented each other in the best ways.

"I know she loves me, Tommy," he said. "But forever is a long time, and what if love isn't enough?"

Well, fuck. I didn't know what to say to that. His parents, by all accounts, didn't have a great marriage. I was fairly certain that my parents only stayed together because of us kids. Neither of us had any idea how marriage should look from the inside.

I got up and walked over to where he stood, looking out the window into the side yard where wedding guests were taking their seats. "Well... In the wise and careful words of Smokey from Friday's mama, make it enough."

Jared barked out a surprised howl of laughter. "I can't fucking stand you, Tomás."

"You lie. You fucking love me, bro. Now put on your jacket. It's time to get you married."

The main floor of Darcy's Charleston single had been transformed. Plumeria, lilies, and roses, the scents of which hung thickly in the air, lined the hallways and the piazzas. A string quartet played God Only Knows out there, and well-dressed guests made their way to the side yard where the ceremony would take place. I didn't know if it was the heady perfume of the flowers, the sticky, cool breeze blowing in off the river, or just that Charleston ambience, but everything took on this dream-like quality. Surreal but familiar in the way that things I'd only witnessed but had never been a part of could be. The rings in my breast pocket suddenly felt heavy and precious, and not because of their combined weight, but heavy with significance and symbolism.

The rest of the groomsmen were already escorting various guests to their seats as needed. How they managed to look halfway human after last night was a miracle. Jared found the wedding planner and greeted him with a big smile.

"Look at you two! You clean up nice! And punctual! We have about seven minutes before we need to get everyone in place. Tomás, you're supposed to escort Jared's mother down the aisle. Right?"

"Yup. I've got Darcy. I need to give Brandi your wedding gift anyway."

"Right, right. Thanks, Tomás," he murmured, taking the jewelry box out of his breast pocket.

My heart skipped like an excited kid as I made my way upstairs. The boy in me wanted to break into a run, but somehow, I managed to cover the distance in measured steps. I hadn't seen or spoken to Darcy since our moment this morning in the laundry room, which I understood rationally wasn't a long time, but it felt like an eternity. As I took the corner at the top of the stairs and went down the hallway to her bedroom, I was reminded of last night. Of Darcy, a wild storm of emotions barely contained within her skin as she took what she needed from me. Would she be that way tonight? *God, I hope so.*

Standing in front of the door, I heard giggles and coos — Brandi and her bridesmaids were using Darcy's room to get ready. James and her glam squad had been hard at work before me and the boys left to go to the barbershop. If those delighted sounds were an indication, the bride was definitely pleased. I rapped on her closed bedroom door and took a step backward.

A few seconds later, James opened the door, and when she saw that it was me, her pretty face split into one of her infamous sultry smiles. "Hey, Tommy."

"Hey, Auntie."

She rolled her eyes and gave a little sigh like she knew it was never going to happen between us, and I laughed because I was flattered. "What's up?"

"I need Darcy." *Wow, that statement feels more true than it should.* "The ceremony is about to start, and I'm supposed to escort her to her seat."

"Come on in. Darcy and Brandi are out on the piazza with the photographer."

As I followed her through the door, I understood why Jared asked me to stay away from his Auntie. James was gorgeous. She was tall and slim, like her sister. Had the same bright copper brown eyes and luminous reddish-toned skin. But there was also something mean about her. Like she'd kiss you with a razor blade tucked behind her bottom lip. Don't get me wrong, that definitely had its appeal, but I just didn't see it for her. Not the way I did for Darcy.

The photographer was capturing a staged but tender moment between Darcy and her soon-to-be daughter-in-law. Brandi was all done up in a dress that made her look like a cupcake — frothy and covered in confectioner's sugar. Jared was gonna fall over when he saw her.

"Tomás!" Brandi exclaimed, dabbing at her eyes. "Is it time already?"

"Almost! I'm here to collect the mother of the groom and to give you this—"

"Is that Jared's wedding gift?" the photographer asked.

"Uh...yeah?"

"Don't give it to her yet. I want to get some shots of you handing it to her and her opening it." All at once, the photographer grabbed me, positioned me opposite Brandi, and took a couple of test shots.

Jared and I had spent most of yesterday afternoon looking for the perfect gift for Brandi. I'd given him all sorts of lists and articles for him to reference, but in the end, he'd settled on something she could wear every day: a gold bracelet fashioned to look like a stethoscope that, when clasped, looked like an infinity sign. It seemed a bit cheesy and on the nose to me, but Jared swore she would love it.

I reached into my breast pocket and pulled out the card and the jewelry box, carefully avoiding the rings tied together with a piece of ribbon — and the condoms I'd stowed in there for later. Brandi looked up at me, tears already welling in her eyes.

"So, who picked this out for me?" she asked playfully, well aware of the dynamic between me and her husband. She knew he wasn't the thoughtful type and was totally okay with the fact that he relied on me to help him buy her birthday and Christmas gifts. She'd even shared her bridal Pinterest board with me when they started talking about marriage to make sure he bought the right ring.

"You know me. I planned everything, and I had a list of things he could choose from, but he chose this all on his own."

"Oh, lord," she said, rolling her eyes. "What's in here?"

"Read the card first."

She narrowed her eyes at me again as she tore open the envelope.

"I don't know what's in the card. He delivered it to me sealed."

I watched her pull the card out of the envelope and begin to read. As her eyes dashed across the heavy cardstock, tears spilled down her cheeks, ruining her makeup. I had no idea what was in that card, but Jared must've done good.

"I love that big-headed boy," she blubbered while opening the small jewelry box. And when she saw the bracelet? She lost it. The photographer captured every moment.

After I helped her put on the bracelet, James swooped in to touch up her makeup. The rest of the bridesmaids crowded around Brandi to coo and swoon over her gift and Jared's message in the card. I finally turned back to Darcy. She was looking at Brandi, a sweet but sort of sad smile on her lips, and her eyes twinkled brightly with unshed tears. My chest clenched tight the moment her eyes met mine, that same sensation of not being able to breathe that overcame me last night.

No one would accuse Darcy of trying to upstage the bride. The dress was demure but so sheer and so close to her skin tone that it seemed as if she had grown a protective gossamer layer filled with twinkling gems that draped over her curves and down to the floor. It was an easy sort of bohemian glamour that was all her, and no other woman downstairs would have been able to pull it off.

"You look stunning," I said breathlessly.

She smiled and ducked her head shyly. "The old lady cleans up nice, huh?"

"You're no old lady, Darcy." Realizing that someone might overhear me, I leaned in and whispered in her ear. "Would an old lady come the way you did on this porch last night?"

A soft gasp made her chest rise and fall sharply. "I guess not," she said, the corners of her mouth twitching into a secret smile as her skin flushed enticingly under the muted but glamorous makeup she had on.

I stepped back and offered my elbow. "Shall we?"

"Let's!" She giggled girlishly and took my arm.

12

DARCY

Tommy slowed his pace once we reached the hallway outside of my bedroom. When I closed the door behind us, and the tinkling of female laughter faded, he crowded both of us behind a big potted rubber tree plant that hid us from the bedroom door and the hallway. His hands settled on my hips, and they felt so hot that I had to look down at them, worried that the delicate fabric hadn't disintegrated under his touch. Drawing the tip of his nose up the line of my neck, he whispered, "Can I kiss you?"

"Not on the lips. James spent hours on this makeup, and she'd murder me if I smudged it."

He huffed out a growl of frustration then placed a soft, wet kiss just under my chin. "I guess I'll just have to be patient and wait for our appointment then."

"I guess we both will," I whispered back, my body heating at the thought of finally slaking the intense need that had grown between us. I only hoped that one night would be enough. Not that it really mattered. He was still my son's best friend. Nothing could come of this thing between us. By this time tomorrow, Tommy would be back in Chicago.

"We should get downstairs," I said, pushing him away.

Tommy searched my face, a crinkle between his brows. "What's wrong?"

"Nothing!" I squeaked a little too excitedly. "I just don't want to hold up the ceremony."

He stared into my eyes for a long moment, then checked his watch. "You're right. I should get you to your seat."

Quickly, but taking care not to rush me too much, Tommy helped me navigate my way through the house toward my seat on the groom's side.

I could see the back of Jolene's head as we made our way down the aisle. I clenched my teeth and bit back the nasty remark that nearly passed my lips. But I must have made some sort of sound because Tommy covered the hand I had in the crook of his arm with his own.

"Twenty minutes. You only have to sit next to her for twenty minutes, and then I'll rescue you," he whispered as we neared my seat.

I didn't know if he meant it as a joke, but I was suddenly so immensely grateful that he'd stepped in to take care of me during this ceremony. "Thank you, Tommy."

He gave me one of his wicked lopsided grins. "My pleasure. I'm at your service, remember?" he said, then dropped a hand to my waist and held the chair steady as I sat down.

Jolene glanced my way as I made myself comfortable. "Good evening, Darcy," she said haltingly.

"Jojo," I returned curtly.

Jolene was wearing a slip of a dress, seemingly made of the leftovers from a real garment meant to cover someone's body. She crossed her bare legs and angled them in a way that elongated them. "You look lovely, Darcy. Mother of the bride dresses always look so matronly to me, but not on you," she said.

I rolled my eyes and chuckled at her weak attempt to bait me into a sniping match. "Thanks," I said, accepting her back-handed compliment. I knew I didn't look matronly. The way Tommy was still staring at me validated that in ways that no one else could.

"Thomas certainly is taking that concierge duty seriously, isn't he?" Jolene said. "He has always been overly fond of you."

"His name is *Tomás*," I ground out between clenched teeth. "And what do you mean, overly fond?"

"Just that Shannon told me that he was always sniffing around your skirts. Flirting shamelessly and being overly helpful and all that. It's just the first time I've seen it in action. It's cute, but I hope you're not taking it seriously."

"Taking what seriously?" I asked quietly, feeling hurt and anger rise in me just as quietly at his implication.

"Well, all of the attention he's giving to you. He's a good-looking kid, and I can understand how that kind of attention can boost your ego—"

"I'm sure you can," I interrupted, giving her pointed look.

Jolene chuckled, completely unfazed and not at all embarrassed. "I'm just saying, a young, successful man like that has his choice of women at a wedding. It was chivalrous of him to volunteer to take care of you, but you should release him from those duties so the boy can have some fun."

I narrowed my eyes at my dead husband's smug mistress wearing that self-satisfied smirk. I knew bourbon was probably the reason she took that jab at me. Why she wanted to cut me down to size. I wished I could pinpoint when or why being graceful and taking her circumstances into consideration wasn't enough for her to be less bitter and spiteful. Maybe it was because she struggled once he was gone. Maybe she thought all of the money was his and she would get the big chunk of it, which would have never been the case because the money was always mine, not his. Either way, she felt the need to snipe at me this way more and more often, which was why I'd limited my interactions with her. But this... this need to make me feel small and unwanted on my son's wedding day? A day when it should be easy to be cordial with each other? I didn't understand it. It was mean and spiteful in a way that I just couldn't wrap my head around.

I refused to respond to it, though. Refused to give her that energy.

Instead, I canted my body so I didn't have to see or acknowledge him, took my hand fan out of the little pearl clutch that I'd paired with my matronly dress, and proceeded to kick up enough wind to keep my immaculately applied makeup from succumbing to the heat and humidity of the day.

"Darcy, there's no need to get sensitive. I'm just stating—"

"Shhh! My son is coming down the aisle!" I hissed through clenched teeth.

And damn was he a good-looking kid. He had my coloring but his father's height and aquamarine eyes. His hair was like mine and leaned toward a sandy, reddish brown in the summer. He was thirty-two years old. He'd been a grown man for a long time, but as I watched him make his way down the aisle, I saw none of my little boy in him.

That melancholy feeling that came over me yesterday afternoon swelled in me again as he came to stand over me. "You look gorgeous, ma," he whispered, then leaned in to kiss me on the cheek.

He didn't even smell like my boy anymore. I gave him a wobbly smile when he pulled away.

"Don't cry, mama. It's a happy day."

"I know," I whispered hoarsely. So why did I feel this loss so keenly? "I'm just so happy for you," I said, patting his cheek. "She's beautiful, and I know that the two of you will be happy together."

My boy grinned and loped to his place near the pastor. Tommy followed, his gaze focused on me.

"You okay?" he mouthed, then gestured toward his pocket, where I knew he probably had another one of those handkerchiefs.

I gave him a polite smile and nodded. He returned the nod and added a wink for good measure. A wink delivered with a look that said he was looking forward to our appointment tonight.

But Jolene's words rang in my ears too. And they stuck with me all the way through the twenty-one-minute ceremony. My son blubbered through his vows — most of which he forgot — and ended inelegantly with, "I love you so much. I love everything about you. The way you move. The way you speak. The way you eat." That got him lots of laughs, but it made me wonder if anyone had ever felt that way about me? Had Shannon?

They kissed — boy, did they kiss. I couldn't remember Jared ever kissing someone the way he kissed his new wife in front of me. It made that old adage seem even more true. A son's a son 'til he takes a wife, but a daughter is a daughter all her life.

I had no daughters. Jared was my only son. And I was losing him to a beauty in a frothy white dress with a hard Northern accent and a look for him like he hung the moon. I wanted to be happy for them — I *was* happy for them. But I couldn't help feeling sad for myself.

Jared and Brandi jumped the broom, and the string quartet played a peppy version of Beyoncé's Love on Top as they made their way back down the aisle, followed by the wedding party. As he passed, Tommy leaned in and whispered, "Stay there. I'll come back for you," then made his way to the reception area with one of Brandi's bridesmaids on his arm.

Next to me, Jolene tsked and pushed herself into an

upright position. "I think this is the perfect time to get myself another drink," she announced he while aiming a smug smile at me.

I didn't try not to roll my eyes this time. I refused to say I hated this. Refused to let her have that much power over me or rent that space in my head to her for free. However, I was creeping toward strong dislike. Maybe even loathing.

I was still considering that whilst staring daggers at her back when Tommy reappeared. He stood over me, hands shoved into the pockets of his tux.

"Hey, Darcy," he said in a low sensual voice that licked against my damp skin.

"You came back to rescue me," I said, smiling up at him before I stood and took his arm.

"Of course, I did, hermosa. I promised you I would, didn't I?"

I nodded and focused my attention on the garden pavers under my feet. "You did, but... I just want to reiterate that this was a good and chivalrous thing you agreed to do, but if you want to—"

"Are you kidding me right now?" His steps slowed to a stop, and he turned toward me. We were still a good distance from the rest of the wedding guests, who were milling about on the piazza and around the pool enjoying cocktails. Still, it felt like everyone's eyes were on us.

"Tell me you're not trying to get rid of me when I have been looking forward to this all damn day."

That declaration made an involuntary smile come to my lips. "There are a lot of pretty girls here, Tommy. Single girls. I know you said—"

"Darcy, I don't want to spend the evening with some random pretty, single girl." His voice dropped into a low, urgent tone. "Why this sudden change of heart? Do you want to...cancel our appointment?"

I looked up at him. Looked into his eyes. "You still want that?"

"Yes," he answered before I finished asking the question. "I've been thinking about being inside of your tight, wet pussy all day, Darcy. Yes. Yes, I still want that. Still want *you*."

Still want you. Not just anyone. He wanted me. "Okay," I whispered, still stunned and confused by all of this. Confused by the fact that he wanted me this way. Stunned by how intensely I wanted him in return.

"Hmmm... Darcy," he moaned, closing his eyes. "Please, take my arm so I can escort you to the bar before I end up on my knees worshiping your pussy again."

I gasped at the intense and immediate arousal I felt as I recalled his mouth on my pussy this morning.

"Yup. You're definitely going to sit on my face tonight. Definitely," he said with a nod. "But first, drinks."

All through the reception, Tommy stuck close to my side, just like he promised. He kept my glass full, danced with me. Jumped up to pull out my chair or provide an elbow for balance the moment I appeared to need it.

"You are going to make some woman very happy," my sister James said as we all stood to say goodbye to the newlyweds. "I wish that woman could be me," she added with a wistful sigh.

Tommy gave her an assessing look that swept from her face down to the curve of her ass. "If you apply yourself, I'm sure there are plenty of young men here who would be willing to make you happy. At least for the night."

James threw a sassy look over her shoulder. "That's all I would want, anyway."

"Hm...is that a fact?" Carter asked, sliding in and looping an arm around her waist.

"Oh! Where have you been all night?" James received him with such surprised enthusiasm that Tommy and I had to laugh.

Outside on the stoop, we threw rose petals and held sparklers to light the way to the limo for the newlyweds. That pang of melancholy swept through me again when Jared turned and looked right at me to blow me a kiss and say goodbye. I've always been the sentimental type, but this felt like it was hitting me harder than usual.

When the couple was finally on their way to the hotel for their honeymoon, and the guests had said their goodbyes, I made my way back into the reception room.

The caterers were making short work of breaking down the tables and sweeping up the glitter and confetti on the floor. The party always looked tired and deflated after the guests were gone, but something about this room felt particularly flat tonight.

"You planned a really beautiful wedding and reception, Darcy."

I shrugged and hugged myself. "I wanted it to be special for Brandi and Jared."

"I think it was," he said softly.

"Didn't you ask me for a kiss earlier?" I asked, turning to him as he made his way across the room to where I stood.

"I did."

"Do you still want one?" I asked, giving him my best saucy grin.

"I do," he said with a soft moan and slow smile. "But I think you need something first."

"What?"

"Hold on a second." He looked around the room, spotted the stereo system and the shelf full of records, and strode toward it confidently. Flipping through the records, he plucked one from the shelf that had a familiar cover and placed it carefully on the turntable. As he made his way toward me with a smile on his face, the first chords of

Dinah Washington's What a Difference a Day Makes began to play.

A smile spread across my face as he took me in his arms and began to sway.

"This is one of your favorite songs, isn't it?"

"Yes, how did you know?"

"You played it all the time when I lived here with you."

"Hm," I hummed, leaning my head against his shoulder. "You remember that?"

"I remember lots of things, Darcy." His arms encircled me, holding me against him as he rocked and twirled me around the room. "Are you okay?"

"Yeah," I answered reflexively.

"I don't think that's true. I know you've been holding it in all night. You can let it go now, hermosa."

Almost on cue, the tears came. It wasn't like they had far to go. They were right under the surface all day, weren't they? "I don't know why I'm so sad. I love my son, and I'm so happy that he's found someone to love, but...all of it makes me feel so empty."

"This is a big transition, and he's your only son. It's perfectly normal to mourn that."

I clung to him, and Tommy just held me. He just gave me something to hold onto. I was so glad he was here. Glad that I didn't have to go through this by myself. He pressed sweet kisses against my temple and along my neck. I tipped my head back to look him in the eyes.

"Thank you," I whispered.

He shook his head, a wrinkle forming between his brows. "You don't have to thank me, Darcy."

"I know. But you didn't have to be so good to me tonight. So sweet." I brought up a hand to cup his cheek, and he nuzzled into the touch.

"Hm. I tried. Can I have my kiss now? Have I been good enough?"

I laughed, but the sound was deep and unfamiliar to me, like a laugh that belonged to someone else. Maybe it did. "Yes, Tommy. You can have your kiss now."

The first brush of his lips was hesitant. The next, searching, teasing with a nibble at my bottom lip so that I gasped and opened my mouth to him. "Darcy," he whispered between soft, sucking kisses. "You shouldn't feel empty. Not tonight. Not when I'm here to fill you up."

13

DARCY

A strange feeling rose in me as we climbed the stairs to my bedroom. It was familiar, but it had been a long time since I felt it. The last time I'd felt this way was with Shannon after I found out about his first affair. He'd been weepy and apologetic. I was sad and angry, more angry than I had ever been or had been since. I'd felt like I needed to reclaim him. To erase any invisible evidence that other woman had left on his body. He was willing to let me use him to take the edge of my anger. And at the time, it had a cleansing effect, and we were able to move on...for a little while.

I wasn't angry tonight, though.

Tonight, I was spurred on by the uncommon lust inspired by the pretty young man climbing the stairs behind me. I wanted to leave bruises and bites on all the tender parts of him.

We climbed the stairs and walked down the hallway in silence. The moment the door was closed behind us, I came at him with my mouth. Took ownership of his lips and tongue in a way that I knew would leave them swollen and raw when I was done. He moaned into it, hands coming around my waist. I pushed those hands away and proceeded to separate him from his clothes.

His lovely tuxedo jacket hit the floor first. When I grabbed the hem of his shirt, he lifted his arms to ease its path over his shoulders because I was too eager to undo more than four buttons. My hands didn't shake or fumble like I thought they would when I reached for his belt. I felt none of my earlier nervousness as I unzipped his fly. I pushed his slacks down around his ankles while feathering kisses over his lower belly. When I curled my fingers around the elastic waistband of his briefs and yanked them down, his cock leaped free, and I graced it with a tiny kiss. He smiled down at me, and oh, god, it sent a spike of arousal through me so strong that it made me dizzy. What the fuck was this feeling? It had to be the knowledge that, at this moment, he would let me do anything to him. Anything at all.

I stood slowly, ghosting my breath over his skin so that goosebumps rose.

"Darcy..." he breathed.

The sound of his voice when he said my name in that ragged, desperate way... I was definitely getting way too fond of that.

There was barely a breath between us, and I could tell everything in him ached to close it. As much as I wanted to, I didn't give in. I let him sway in the space, begging me with every inch of him to come closer. I didn't relent. But finally, *finally*, he did. Without a single word, Tommy sank to his knees.

Why would he do that?

And god, why the fuck did that make everything in me feel greedy and grabby? It shrunk him down to my size — smaller, even. Made me feel stronger than I was when I walked through the door. His hands slid under my dress, bunching the heavy beaded fabric to cup my ass, as he burrowed his face into the place just beneath my breasts. I sifted my fingers through the soft curls on the crown of his head. He sighed and trembled against me.

"You can use me," he said, his voice muffled against the fabric of my dress.

I knew exactly what he was suggesting, and it scared me shit-less. I couldn't breathe. I couldn't do anything but cradle his head against my breasts as I struggled to understand the feelings his words had evoked.

"Use me, Darcy." He looked up at me, dark brown eyes framed in wispy, black lashes. "Don't be afraid of it. I'm not."

My toes curled in my heels, anxiously gripping for purchase because this wonky, woozy feeling was surely some sort of seismic activity shifting the floor under my feet. It couldn't be my heart pounding so violently that it made my whole body quake. He closed his eyes for a moment, his hands gripping tighter on the back of my thighs.

"Please, Darcy."

I took a deep breath and slid my hands down to his shoulders. "Take off my panties." He pushed my heavy beaded dress higher, eager fingers tugging at the waistband of the scrap of lace covering my pussy. "Slowly!" I hissed.

And damn if he didn't do it just right.

He dragged my panties down a millimeter at a time, finger-tips igniting every nerve ending from my pussy to the backs of my knees. When they were crumpled around my ankles, he took the time to remove each of my shoes. Without being asked, he traced the space between my toes with his tongue. My pussy pulsed tightly like I was on the brink of orgasm.

He smiled up at me before sucking a toe between his kiss-swollen lips. *Yup.* The fucker knew exactly what he was doing.

I put my foot in the middle of his chest and pushed him backward. He didn't even try to check his fall, just hit the hardwood floor with a thud. He stared up at me, eyes gone glassy and hooded with want. One hand slid down the length of his torso to fit around his dick.

I tsked and waggled my finger. "Did I tell you to touch it?"

A laugh or sneer or some sort of rude retort was what I expected, but instead, he nodded, picked up his belt from where he'd tossed it aside, and fed the end through the buckle until he'd made it into two loops. He slipped his hands through those two loopholes then used his teeth to pull the tail tight, effectively handcuffing himself. With a smirk, he raised his hands above his head. Seeing him like that — prone, naked, and helpless on the floor — it did things to me.

I hiked up my dress, exposing my pussy, wet and meant for his mouth, and walked up the length of him. When my feet were even with his shoulders, I stopped. His eyes immediately focused between my legs, so attentive and direct that I could feel it, and when he pursed his lips, my clit gave a quick twitch in response.

Deep breath in... Drawing in the scents of the magnolias from the tree just beyond the open piazza doors and him. He smelled like a blend of leaves and woods, a sweet, smoky tobacco aroma layered over a salty, robustly male smell that would probably be in my sheets when he left. *Slow, cleansing breath out...* Sinking down to my knees, bringing my pussy within inches of his lips. Tommy craned his neck to cover the rest of the distance between his mouth and my pussy. One broad lick of his tongue made my thighs quiver. The second lick loosened my hips, and I sank down, covering his mouth. His tongue pushed inside of me. Penetrated just enough to make my inner walls contract. I rocked my hips and accidentally caught my clit on the edge of his teeth in such a way that it released something wild in me. Suddenly, I was on the brink of coming, and he ceased to be Tommy and became this thing, this being only meant to bring me off. I grabbed his bound hands and used them as leverage as I rolled my hips against his mouth, reveling at the combined feel of his stubble-rough cheeks and eager sucking. He groaned, and his tongue wandered lower before fucking into my pussy again. His mouth made hungry, wet sounds against my skin. The sound of him going at me so greedily pushed me right over the edge.

"Oh, shit!" I cursed breathlessly, and everything in me clutched tightly in a series of spasms that weakened me until I collapsed, my cheek pressed against the gritty floor.

I would have never thought it was possible, but this orgasm was better than the last.

It was strange, but in my sex-drunk haze, the first thought that came to my mind was Shannon. I wished he'd been here to witness this. Wished he could witness someone fulfilling desires that he was certain I no longer had.

Belatedly, I realized that I might be smothering Tommy or drowning him or both, and was proved right when he took a great big gasping breath when I rolled off of him.

"Sorry!" I said breathlessly.

"Hmm...don't be," he panted, trying to catch his breath. "It was amazing. You were amazing." He made another contented humming sound and smacked his lips. I opened my eyes. His face was a mess — the remnants of my orgasm were all over it. My eyes drifted lower down to his chest, which expanded and contracted at a quick pace, but that wasn't what drew my attention. There, just above his navel, was the evidence of his own orgasm.

"Tommy..." I trailed my fingers through the slippery fluid and frowned. His hands were bound the whole time. I was sure of it because they were still bound. Yet there it was, cooling on his belly when neither of us had touched his dick. "You came."

His mouth slanted into a crooked smile. "Yeah, I did."

"But how? Your hands were tied the whole time, and I didn't touch you."

"I don't know." He shrugged. "I just did."

"Huh," I grunted.

He opened one eye and peeked at me. "Maybe it's time we had a conversation about my...kinks."

"Your...kinks?" I questioned in the same halting way he'd said the word.

He licked his lips. "Let's get in the shower and get cleaned up so we can chat about it."

TOMMY HAD SUGGESTED A SHOWER, but I felt like a bath was more appropriate for a conversation like this. He agreed and immediately went in to fill the tub. Balanced on the edge of my big copper soaker tub, he looked like a painting of a young boy in a Grecian bathhouse with his hand in the stream of water and his legs crossed just so, hiding his dick from view.

"Is this warm enough, hermosa?" he asked.

On legs still wobbly from coming so hard, I went to stand next to him and tested the water. "It's perfect."

"Do you want a bath bomb or bubbles or oils or anything?"

"Just you."

Tommy looked up at me, and in this light, I could see that his pupils were so blown that he looked high. I smoothed back his mussed hair and pressed a kiss between his brows.

"Help me out of this dress."

He stood and gestured for me to turn around. Heavy and already halfway hard, his dick drew my attention. "You have to turn around for me to get the zipper, hermosa," he said with a chuckle.

I twisted my lips to hide my smirk as I turned around. "Hermosa...what's that mean?"

"Hermosa?" He gathered my hair and pulled it over my shoulder, then tugged the zipper down slowly, so slowly while letting out a soft moan as he revealed my bare skin. "Beautiful. Hermosa means beautiful."

"Hermosa," I echoed.

"Roll the 'r' a little bit more," he whispered, his lips brushing against the skin at the nape of my neck.

I shivered and stuttered the word out again, butchering it in a way I didn't the first time, which made him laugh, a breathy sound that I felt in the same spot he'd left his kiss. He followed it with another, then pushed the dress over my shoulders. I curled them forward and straightened my arms, sending the beads and sequins held together by gossamer threads to the floor in a whispering heap.

And then I was naked in front of him. Again. But this time, we were naked together, and I could feel the heat of his bare skin against my back.

I turned to him, and the tip of his now completely hard length brushed along my hip, leaving a thin strip of moisture in its wake. The incidental contact made him gasp. I reached for him, and he caught both my hands at the wrists and pulled them down to my sides.

"Darcy, I'm dying to be inside of you. I think that's pretty fucking obvious. But I feel like it's important for this conversation to happen first." He placed a soft kiss to my lips and then stepped into the tub and held out a hand, silently asking me to join. Anxious and a little frustrated, I took it and sank down into the water. It was just this side of hot, and we both grunted then sighed with contentment as we settled into the healing warmth — me at one end and him at the other. He parted his muscular thighs, gathered my feet into his lap, and began to massage my sore soles.

"This is nice," he murmured, his eyes and attention focused on making concentric circles on the arches of both feet.

"It is. If I knew this came with a foot massage, I would have given in to your flirtatious behavior a lot sooner."

"Hm," he grunted, then lifted my foot out of the water and pressed his lips to that sensitive arch. "If you need or want a foot massage, you only need to ask."

"Okay," I murmured, sinking lower into the tub and parting my legs, slipping my hand between them because feeling his lips on a place so often ignored made me want to have them on my pussy again. "Is that your kink? Kissing and massaging my feet? If a foot fetish is the extent of your kinks, Tommy, I have to say that you're making much too big of a deal of this."

He looked up at me from under his thick, dark lashes. Had I ever noticed how dark and lovely his lashes were before tonight? Maybe I was just noticing how lovely Tommy was, period.

"I don't have a foot fetish, Darcy. It's more like I have a *you* fetish...are you playing with your pussy right now?"

"Yes."

"That's my job," he said, a determined frown creasing his brow. "Come 'ere."

Water sloshed as I crawled over to his side of the tub. He pulled my back against his chest. The hard length of his dick pressed against my spine for one glorious moment before he adjusted himself into what I presumed was a more comfortable position.

"Show me," he whispered, grasping my inner thighs and hooking my knees over his. "Show me how you make yourself come. I wanna know exactly how you do it."

The little waves I'd made while moving to his side of the tub buffeted against my sensitive pussy. "You already know how."

"Mm," he hummed thoughtfully. "Not really. I know you like it when I have my fingers inside of you and make you squirm in my lap. I know you like it when you're sitting on my face, and you roll your hips up just enough for me to tongue, taste, and lick your ass, but I don't know how you make yourself come."

My pussy tightened around the emptiness I wanted him to fill.

"Show me, hermosa," he whispered in my ear, an edge of desperation in his voice as if he needed to touch me as much as I needed to be touched.

I took his left hand in mine and placed it in between my thighs. The moment his hand made contact with my pussy, he slipped two of his thick fingers inside of me in one quick stroke.

"Hey!" I said, scolding him lightly but also moaning because it felt so damn good.

"Sorry," he whispered, his fingers still inside of me.

"I'm supposed to be showing you how I make myself come."

"I know, but damn. You don't know how good you feel, flaca. So hot and tight...just feeling you on my fingers makes me want to come." He rocked his hips ever so slightly against my back, and his dick throbbed where he had it pinned between us.

"Me first," I panted, covering his hand with my own.

"*Always.* You come first always," he whispered passionately, then withdrew his fingers slowly, and I flexed those intimate inner muscles, squeezing them on his retreating digits. He grunted, and his hips gave a hard involuntary thrust, sloshing water out of the tub.

"Damn...okay. Show me," he murmured in a rush.

I positioned his fingers right over my clit. The contact made me shiver, and a delicious rush of pleasure arrowed through my core. "Just your fingertips. Right there."

"Right here?" he whispered, his fingers pressing lightly in the right spot, the perfect spot.

"Yes, yes, yes. Oh, god. Right there, Tommy. But soft and slow... Soft, slow circles!" I panted.

"Like this?" he asked, and goddamnit, he did it just right, and it felt so damn good that my eyes rolled back in my head.

"Mmm... yes," I moaned. His touch was so perfect and so good that I almost wanted to run away from it, but when I tried to clench my legs together, I realized that he had my thighs pinned to the sides of the tub with his own.

"*Shitshitshitshit*," I cursed, digging my fingers into his thighs.

"This is it, Darcy. This is my kink. *You*. Making you come. You letting me give you pleasure. Worshiping your pussy in any and every way you ask...that's it. That's what does it for me. As much as I'm aching to be inside of you? Fuck, this is enough. Being inside of you is the bonus, baby. Making you come, it's enough."

"Yes, please. Make me come," I moaned, only partially hearing what he said.

"Tell me what you need right now," he demanded.

"Just straight up and down strokes."

"Like this?" he asked, angling his fingers.

"Yes!" It was so good that my abdominal muscles clenched, making my back arch. "Yes! Just like that...just...just like that," I stammered.

Tommy gripped my inner thigh with his other hand, squeezing and massaging it with his strong fingers, then slid lower to play with my pussy lips.

"Too much. It's too...oh! Please!" I begged, unsure if I was begging him to stop or begging my body to come because dangling on the precipice felt so good that it hurt.

"Go ahead and come, hermosa. I'm right here."

I took a deep breath and let it out slowly, a weak attempt to let go, but it was just enough for the orgasm to unfurl slowly in little waves then slam through me. "Tommy...oh, god!"

"Fuck...that's magic," he whispered. "Shit. I'm coming

again...this...this doesn't make any sense," he moaned, his mouth pressed against my shoulder and both of his arms wrapped around me.

It took an embarrassingly long time for my hips to stop fucking into the empty place between my thighs. It was an eternity before I finally went limp and boneless in his embrace.

We were both dazed and panting from our release, but it was that one thing — knowing that he came again without my hands on him, without touching him — that made the words he'd whispered in my ear while he was playing with my pussy make sense.

This is it. This is my kink, Darcy. You. Making you come. It took a moment, but my mind pieced together what he was trying to say. "You're submissive."

"Yes," he said, giving my sides an eager squeeze. "And you're dominant."

"I... I never...you think so?"

"Yes. I know so." He groaned and hugged me tighter, gripping my sides in his big hands. "Now that we have all of that out of the way, can you please use me? I'm fucking dying for it."

14

TOMÁS

How I could be so relieved yet feel still so raw and vulnerable didn't make much sense to me. Telling Darcy that I was submissive and that most of my submissive fantasies were about her made it difficult to speak as we made short work of bathing and then toweling each other dry before moving back into her bedroom. She went to her vanity — a glass and brass table and mirror in the corner of her room where she grabbed a bottle of oil. The smell was familiar, wholly hers with some note in it that reminded me of church and the haunting sound of mass recited in Latin by a chorus of male voices.

"Let me do that," I asked softly, and she smirked before handing the bottle to me.

I pulled out the little bench for the vanity, sat, and motioned for her to come close. Darcy stepped into the space between my knees and placed her hands on my shoulders.

After pouring a generous amount of oil into my palm, I began to massage it into her still damp skin. I started with her calves, working them with my thumbs until the tight muscles loosened, then moved up to her thighs, struggling not to pay too close attention to the crease between her thigh and her pussy, which was distractingly soft and inviting and made her moan and whimper. Her breasts were right at eye level, though, and I couldn't help nuzzling against them and drawing my lips across her dark cherry nipples as I worked the oil into her skin, making it glow in the muted, intimate light her bedside lamps cast around the room.

Darcy sighed and hugged me to her chest. "What are we doing, Tommy?" she whispered in my ear.

What are we doing?

Making my heart want things I can't possibly have. Binding myself to you in a way that's probably going to feel like dying when I walk away.

"We're making each other feel good for the next eighteen hours," I said finally.

"Eighteen hours," she echoed softly. "Is that all we have?"

"Yeah."

"And then we'll pretend like this never happened."

I wrapped my arms around her, buried my face in the soft, sweet pillow of her breasts. It wasn't a question, but I answered it anyway. "Yes...then I'll pretend that it never happened. Pretend that I've never tasted you. Never heard you moan my name. Pretend I don't know how you look and feel when you come."

Darcy stepped back a little and took my face in both her hands. Looked me in the eyes. "I shouldn't do this to you. I know it's wrong."

"Is it wrong?" I asked with a shrug of my shoulders. "If we'd met any other way, you and I, me wanting you, wouldn't be a problem. But...there are relationships that are important to us that make it so this can never exist outside of this moment. Even indulging it just this once is probably a bad idea, but..." I drew my hands up the back of her legs, gripped her ass, and slipped my fingers between those pert cheeks to find her wet slit, skim across her pinched tight exit, make her gasp. "There's no way I'm giving up the next eighteen hours."

I stood and tucked my hands under her arms, lifting her into the air. She wrapped her legs, arms, everything around me as I carried her over to her bed.

"I'm gonna dive face-first into every single one of my fantasies."

"How dirty are these fantasies?" she asked as she peppered my lips with soft kisses.

"Hm... There's the one where you tie me to your bed and edge me all day but don't let me come until you're good and damn ready. Or the one where I eat your pussy by the pool in the middle of the day where any one of your neighbors or passersby could see. Or maybe one of the ones where you force me into a dark corner or up against the wall and command me to give you pleasure whenever and wherever you need it. But I think, right now... I just want you to use me. Ride me until I beg you to let me come and then use me some more." I yanked the sheets and coverlet off the bed. We had so little time, and I didn't want to waste even a second of it on untangling our limbs from them.

Eighteen hours... I wanted more time, but I knew there was no point in pushing against that boundary. I was lucky to even have this.

I crawled to the middle of the bed on my knees and deposited her gently on the pristine white sheets. Her knees fell wide, and I caught the scent of her arousal — musky, sweet, and still on my tongue. It nearly made me pin her to the bed with my dick.

"Condoms," I gritted out, but not before she lifted her hips, making the tip of my dick skim through her folds, dip into her opening. I fisted my hands in the sheets as she rolled her hips again. "Oh...shit. Condoms, condoms, condoms," I chanted, but it took every bit of my strength to pull away and find my tux jacket and produce the packet of condoms I'd stowed there earlier today.

She watched me with hooded eyes and played with her pussy, slipping her fingers inside as if she couldn't wait to be filled.

Nothing will ever compare to this, I thought, as I made my way back to the bed with the condoms in hand. I tore one from the trio, but my hands were trembling, and I couldn't grasp it to tear it open.

"Here," she said, taking the condoms from me. "Lie down, sweetheart," she said, shifting onto her knees.

Heart nearly taking flight at the soft words and endearment that she used, I did as I was told. Flat on my back, my dick sprang rudely into the empty air. Darcey smiled and wiggled, tucking her feet under her bottom. With a featherlight touch, she stroked one hand from the root of my dick to the tip.

"Fuck, Darcy," I cursed softly, my hips lifting involuntarily to chase her touch.

"Hm...so how does your dirty fantasy go again? I ride this..." She punctuated the word with a firm upward tug on my dick, thumb smearing the precum that spilled from the tip and spreading it over the head.

"Yes," I panted.

"Hm," she hummed again before fitting her lips around the tip of me and giving my dick a soft, sucking kiss. "Can you do that without coming?"

"Shit... Darcy. I don't..." She gave it another kiss, and I melted into the mattress, barely resisting the urge to thrust past her lips. "I don't know, hermosa. I'm gonna try, but I don't know. But my dick is still hard, and I've already come twice tonight. I wanna say it will stay that way until you're done using me."

I had no business speaking so confidently in this moment,

especially when nothing like this had ever happened to my body before. Not alone or with anyone else. But I wanted to believe that me and my body were made to serve her in this way, and if I fell short in some way, I would use my fingers or my tongue to get her off.

"Well… I guess I'll have to test it out and see." She tore the foil packet with her teeth and rolled it on — quick, but with enough care and sensuality to have me lifting my hips, chasing her touch again.

With my dick bobbing and reaching for her between our bodies, Darcy braced herself over me on her hands and knees. "Goddamn, Tommy. You have always been so damn pretty."

"I have?" I asked, basking in this moment of adoration.

"Yes," she said, nuzzling her nose against mine. "You and your rumpled hair, and your sweet smiles, and your *yes, Ms. MacFarlands*. So pretty…" she whispered.

She reached down between us and wrapped her hand around me, held me steady, as she notched me at the opening of her pussy.

*Ohhh…*shit. I was wrong. My heart was pounding, breath soughing from my lungs like I'd just finished a hard run. I was definitely going to come the moment I was inside of her. I could already feel that telltale tingling at the base of my spine.

Darcy placed her hand in the middle of my chest. "Shhh…" she quieted. Her cool palm against my heated skin made it easier for me to take a deep breath and helped me relax a little.

No. Relax was the wrong word.

Surrender.

Surrender was much closer to the feeling that rolled through me as my arms fell to my sides, hands still trembling with the need to hold her, touch her, make her end this torturous moment where my dick was notched at her opening. I wanted to grab her hips and force her down, but that wasn't what I asked for, was it?

She kissed me. Soft, wet kisses that had me lapping hungrily at her mouth and arching upward to taste more of her. To thrust my tongue into that wet heat because I needed to be inside of her in some way as she prolonged this moment. Her pussy made little fluttering, butterfly kisses on the tip of my dick, and I felt a little gush of liquid spill from her and trickle down the length of me.

"Darcy, please. This is more torture than any man can take. Let me, let me in..." I begged the words, strung tight and hoarse with need.

I couldn't hold still like this much longer. My need was so intense that it washed over me in waves that wanted to end in a hard upward thrust that would seat me deep inside of her.

When I thought I couldn't wait a moment longer, she started to slide down my dick, taking me in, inch by slow inch, and I was wrong because this was worse. This slow teasing was worse in the most delicious way. She was searing hot inside, wet, tight heat that sent a shock of pleasure to my balls and up my spine. I fisted my hands in the sheets and willed myself not to come.

Don't come. Don't come now because look at her. Jesus Christ... Darcy's lashes fluttered closed as her pussy engulfed my dick. She went still and just held me there. So deep, inside of her, that the tip of me was snug against her womb, and her pussy rippled and clutched at my dick, and she made sexy, needy little sounds. Her face flushed, and she spread one hand across her lower belly. I covered that hand with my own.

"Tommy," she panted, her voice shaky and full of the same intense emotions that I was feeling, and *holy shit...* What a revelation to know that she felt this moment just as intensely as I did.

"Take your time, hermosa. Go as slow as you need. I've waited this long to be with you. I'm in no rush."

She nodded and shivered, and a tear slipped from the corner of her eye and trickled down to the tip of her nose.

Breathing slow and deep, I slid my palms up her thighs, curved them around her trim waist, and up her sides to cup her breasts. When I stroked my thumbs across her nipples, her hips rolled forward, and she picked up a slow, languid rhythm that had me at the precipice of coming in three strokes. The need was like a rush of tiny pinpricks all over my body, and *fuck...no... not yet, not yet, not yet.*

Darcy shifted forward, bracing herself with one hand by my shoulder, and I rocked upward to meet her hips at the bottom of each stroke. This slow, deep fucking was so good, and apparently, it was exactly what she needed. And she let me know how much when each of my thrusts finished so deep inside of her that it forced out a little whimper. Or maybe that was me. Maybe I was the one making those sounds.

She leaned over me, and her breasts brushed against my chest, adding another layer of sensation. The change in position pressed her clit against my lower belly in a way that made her gasp.

Now I knew I was the one who had whimpered before because the sound she made now as she pushed her hips up and back, practically rutting against me, was nothing like the one I'd heard earlier. Her skin was flushed, lips parted and slightly bruised from kissing, breasts swaying with each excited breath she took, her dark brown nipples puckered with arousal, and *oh, fuck...* I was definitely going to come now.

"Shit, Darcy. Can I come?

"No, not yet." Her voice...a delighted chuckle paired with deep satisfaction that almost did me in.

"Please? Oh, fuck."

If she told me I could come, I couldn't hear her because I was trying so hard not to. All I could feel or even think about was how her pussy clutched at me with each thrust until she came with a primal moan. And damn, her pussy clamped down on me so hard right before her hips jerked to a shuddering stop that made a silent prayer of thanks spill from my mouth. And I don't know how I survived that, but I didn't come. I didn't. I was still hard and throbbing inside of her, but the urgent need to finish had banked a bit.

Darcy collapsed on top of me, panting and humming, a sound that made me feel grateful and godlike at the same time to have done that to her. A thin sheen of sweat coated her skin and mine. This moment was so good, so deliciously good and sticky, messy and wet...so wet where our bodies were joined. I couldn't help flexing my dick inside of her, stimulating her tightly clenched intimate muscles just to hear her gasp.

"You didn't come," she whispered, a note of surprise in her voice.

"You told me I couldn't, so I didn't." But I almost felt like I had — all tingly and floaty and lost in a hazy fog of pure bliss. I wondered for a moment if this was how tantric sex felt. Was this the feeling monks were after? Had I found enlightenment in Darcy's pussy?

I dragged my palms down her back and gripped her ass with both hands. "Can I make you come again?"

"Can you?" she teased, but I could hear the note of doubt in her voice.

"Was I supposed to say, may I make you come again?"

"Hm...yes, you may, if you think you can," she retorted playfully, a sly but doubtful smile on her lips.

"I can," I answered, then rolled us over to get her on her back because she was clearly too spent to ride me again.

Darcy flung her arms wide on the bed and looked up at me,

a happy sex-drunk smile on her face. "Was that as good as your fantasy?"

"Better." I braced myself over her and pulled out of her slowly, drawing a sizzling hiss from her lips. She looked down between our bodies when I began another slow slide inside of her. She looked so small under me. Small, but still stronger than me as she flexed and stretched to take me deeper, hips lifting to meet me and navigate a little circle before she dropped them to the mattress again.

That little move made my fucking head swim. I might be on top, but I wasn't in control. Not even a little bit. Her little body was still hungry and impatient, but she was holding back for some reason. "Be yourself with me, hermosa. Tell me what you need," I whispered.

"Harder," she whispered, pulling her legs up in a way that opened her hips and splayed her knees wide, her whole body spread open to me.

With a groan of surrender and appreciation, I leaned down for a slow, languorous kiss, and her tongue explored mine with slow, insistent demand. Whatever came after this, I would have this memory of her, but for now, I would pin her thighs to the mattress with my hands and fuck her like I was worthy of a woman like her.

I withdrew and slammed inside her so hard it took her breath away.

"Yes," she sighed into my mouth. "Just like that."

I kissed her again, moving my tongue to the same rhythm as my hips. Slow, hard, deep, and with her legs pinned like this, I could feel the moment when she started spinning up, tighter and tighter and so wet that the sound of our bodies coming together and all of our moaning and panting was an obscene soundtrack to the thing growing in my chest.

Pulling back, I thrust inside her a little faster now. And

Darcy... She looked up at me, her mouth open, on a chorus of moans... *Beautiful, beautiful, beautiful.* Almost too hard for me to look at because seeing her so flushed, her needy pussy gripping me every time I pulled out...*fuck.* It was too much, and I...

"Tommy!" My name was a soft gasp on her lips right before her thighs pulled up, and she came again, in intense, rolling waves. And there I was, right behind her, about to break the crest.

"Shit! Can I come, hermosa? Please, fuck. I can't... I can't—"

"Yes, come. You can come, Tommy."

Thank you... I lost my rhythm almost immediately, just became complete sensation and jerky staccato thrusts up into her. I rode the waves she made, but they kept cresting and cresting. I curled myself against her, afraid of the fall because *Jesus...* Just this moment before it felt bigger and better than any other time I did fall. A slow, rolling, belly-clenching tumble that made me let out a hoarse shout and bury my dick even deeper because *holy shit.* Her pussy. I wanted to live there. This was my home now. And she held me. With her arms, and her legs, and her sex, she held me in the most intimate way a woman has ever held me, with her secret muscles drawing every drop of cum out of me.

Nope.

Nothing would be the same after this.

15

TOMÁS

In the morning, I woke like I was coming out of a deep, drugged slumber, eyes sticky, my body pleasantly achy like the day after a hard workout. I stretched and reached to the left of me, expecting to find Darcy, but found cool, empty sheets in the place where her warm, naked body should be.

"Darcy?" I called out, pushing my sore body into a seated position.

The doors to the piazza were open, and a breeze wafted in, stirring the curtains and rustling the leaves of the potted plants inside the room.

"Hermosa?" I threw back the sheets and crossed the room to the open doors, assuming she was out there, drinking coffee or watering her plants. But the piazza was empty, and a quick glance found that the bathroom was empty, too.

Grabbing my tux trousers because they were the only clothing I had in the room, I pulled them on over my bare ass and went to find Darcy.

The door stuck and then banged back against the wall, caught on the cross breeze that rushed through the house from the river. Through the floor-to-ceiling windows along the hallway, I saw that the day was slightly overcast, as if a storm was blowing in. I stood there for a moment and stretched my back a bit more, wondering if her leaving me alone in her bed meant something. With so little time left to spend together, I would've thought she would want to wring pleasure out of every moment the way I did.

The hardwood floors felt warm under my bare feet as I made my way to the stairs. Now that I was standing at the top of them, I could smell that strong dark roast that Darcy favored and hear her humming along with Dinah, who was asking her man to think things over. It was an old recording that made Dinah's voice sound tinny with a bit of vocal fry, but her sorrowful, emotive voice carried the song all the same. Darcy really did love Dinah. It wasn't music from her childhood, though, so I wondered how she got into it. I knew for a fact that she spent her formative years getting weak in the knees with SWV and leaving some young man begging while she left the club with a younger, more handsome version of Shannon MacFarland. Not for the first time, I wondered how he'd won her. They seemed so mismatched.

I was midway down the stairs when Darcy floated into view, wearing one of those silk robes that covered just enough to make a young man such as myself wonder what it was hiding. With a watering can in one hand and a coffee mug in the other, she sang along with Dinah. "I was the arm in your armor. I was the miss in your mistake..."

Holding my breath, I sat down on the step and watched her as she sang and sipped from her coffee while watering her plant babies.

I rested my chin on my hand, content to watch her at a chore that had captivated me for years. Goddamn, but the woman was beautiful. Hair wild, robe slipping from one shoulder, the hastily tied belt that barely held it closed allowed a flash of thigh when she turned toward her heirloom monstera.

"Hello, my monster," she crooned, tipping the big metal watering can to drench its roots. "Which of your babies should we give to Brandi, hm?" She set the can down and touched the large, dark leaves as she spoke. "I know it's tradition, but...maybe we should wait a while. She's the cerebral type, which doesn't mean she won't be nurturing, but..." Darcy let the thought trail off as she stroked a finger down the center of one of the largest leaves.

I hadn't budged an inch, but her focus snapped to the left as if I'd called her name. She smiled, cheeks flushing a dusky pink. "Spying on me?" she asked.

"Not spying. Just watching the woman I adore, being adorable."

Darcy bit her lip and glanced down at her watering can. "Are you hungry? I can make you some breakfast. Anything you want."

"Well... I thought I might make a breakfast of the sweet pussy I ate last night..." Her cheeks blushed even redder. "But, I guess your lemon ricotta pancakes will do."

Darcy looked at me with a shy smile on her lips. "I can do that. You want bacon, too?"

"Yes, please."

"Still so polite and respectful after what we did to each other last night," she said with a wry laugh.

"Last night and early this morning," I corrected, remembering how I'd woken up sometime just after dawn with her warm mouth on me and her muttering something about needing to know how I tasted before I left her, and even though I was exhausted and depleted, I gave her what she needed. And let's be fucking real, I wanted it too. "Anyway..." I said, smirking at her still red cheeks. "Seems like I should be more polite and respectful than usual after last night." I stood and made my way to the bottom of the stairs. I took the mug from her hands and sipped. "Hm. Bourbon? So early?"

"It's not early. It's damn near eleven, sleepyhead."

"Fuck," I cursed, pulling my phone out of my pocket to verify the time. "I didn't realize it was so late."

"What time is your flight?" she asked, turning to make her way back to the kitchen.

"Six forty-five," I answered, my tone somewhat accusatory as I followed her down the front hallway. Why did she let me sleep so fucking long?

"Which means you'll have to be at the airport by four-thirty at the latest. Did you arrange for a car?"

"Yes, it'll be here at four." I clenched my teeth. Why was she acting so perfunctory? Maybe I was projecting, but something felt off about her tone. She'd asked about my flight time and how I was going to get to the airport like I hadn't spent the night making her come and worshiping every inch of her.

"Good. Guess I better get started on breakfast, then!"

Darcy stepped out onto the back porch to empty the watering can. I thrust my hands in my pockets and watched her. Setting the watering can in a little storage closet near the door, she dusted off her hands, turned, and caught me staring again.

"What?" she asked, her smile anxious and hesitant now.

I searched her face, looked her in the eyes. There was so much I wanted to say, but what was the point? I was leaving in a few hours, and then...then, this was never going to happen again. "Can you come here, please?"

She looked down at her hands for a moment as if she were contemplating saying no to my simple request, but then crossed the short distance between us, stopping about a foot away.

"Closer, Darcy," I whispered.

"Tommy—"

"Just bring your body over here...please," I added, trying to soften the demand I had no right to make.

She moved in close. Close enough for me to smell her. Somehow, her scent was more intoxicating this morning. It was her, that expensive body oil, and her sweet sex scent, mingled with mine. I closed my eyes and breathed her in. Pressed a kiss to her forehead. "I know it must be jarring for you to confront this in the bright light of day, but I'm begging you not to push me away right now. Let's stay in this bubble until I leave. Please?"

The tension in her shoulders relaxed, and she sighed. "Okay," she agreed, then looked up at me.

"Thank you," I said, grateful that she didn't put up an argument. Neither of us needed to say those words out loud again. We knew what this was...even if I was having a hard time getting my heart and my body to agree. The look in Darcy's eyes said she was struggling to do the same.

She gave me a sad smile. "Can I have a good morning kiss?"

My yes was delivered to her lips. I slipped my hands out of my pockets and wrapped my arms around her, drawing her body against mine. She moaned softly, welcoming my tongue into her mouth. Coffee, bourbon, and her...a taste I never wanted to forget. I sucked it from her lips and her tongue. Her hands grasped at my shoulders; she wanted me closer. I slipped my hand into her robe — yes, still naked. She growled her soft kitten growl, and I went from halfway hard to I-need-to-be-inside-of-you-right-now in seconds. Darcy reached for the waistband of my pants, but just as she undid the hook and bar closure, my stomach growled.

Loudly.

"Ignore it," I grunted, palming her ass because why would I want to eat when I could have her again instead?

Darcy laughed and pulled away a little. "After the way I used you last night, it would be irresponsible of me not to feed you."

"I'm fine. Use me some more, please. I can eat at the airport—"

"No, Tommy. Let me get some calories in you so that I can fuck you properly before you go." She nuzzled her nose against mine then gave my lips a few more hungry nips before pushing me away.

"Fuck me properly? If last night was how you fuck me improperly, I'll have another serving of that, please."

She rolled her eyes and readjusted her robe to hide the breast I'd bared. "Make yourself a cup of coffee," she said, cinching the belt on her robe tight. "We have time. In fact..." She grabbed her phone from the speaker dock and tapped on the screen before sitting it back on the dock again.

My phone vibrated in my pocket, and I pulled it out. When I saw the alert, I laughed. It was an invitation for a dick appointment an hour and a half from now. I accepted the invitation. Her phone chimed from where it sat in the speaker dock and smiled a secret smile.

"So...lemon ricotta pancakes," she said, heading toward the pantry. "It's been so long since I've made them. I hope I remember the recipe."

I licked my lips, still tasting her, and grabbed a coffee cup out of the cabinet. "Where's the bourbon?"

"In the freezer, sweetheart."

Sweetheart. The endearment warmed me, and in that moment, I decided to indulge in a bit of fantasy.

Darcy re-emerged from the pantry, her arms full of the ingredients for the pancakes. "Could you grab the big mixing bowl from the top shelf in the cabinet by the fridge? Minerva is taller than me, and I swear she puts things where I can't reach just to wind me up."

I went to retrieve the bowl she wanted, feeling her eyes on me the whole time. I'd briefly considered running over to the garçonnière to change, but now I was glad I hadn't. "Where's Minerva this morning?"

"I gave her the day off, so she's spending it with her grandkids."

"Minerva has grandkids?" I asked, setting the bowl on the kitchen island. "Why is that such a surprise to me?"

"Probably because she's here so much you thought she was a live-in. Minerva has been the one constant in my life. I'm so grateful for her." She shook her head and opened the utensil drawer to retrieve measuring spoons and a whisk. "She was there for me when I was a new wife, a new mother, a new widow... Minnie has become a sort of security blanket for me."

I leaned on the counter across from where she was setting up, and her eyes immediately went to my shoulders and my bare chest. Yeah, shirtless was definitely a good decision. "But you and Minnie are close, right? I mean, it's not your typical employer/employee relationship."

Darcy sighed and shrugged. "I like to think it is, but...how can it be? Minnie has put my family ahead of her own for years, and I keep her on even though I don't really need the help because I live alone." She turned to grab eggs, milk, lemons, and ricotta out of the fridge. I didn't cook much, and rarely from scratch, but I realized as she was measuring out the ingredients that she'd bought all of it ahead of time because she knew they were my favorite. She'd planned to make them for me while I was in town. That made me happier than it should.

"So, why do you keep her around?" I asked, trying to hold up my end of the conversation without getting lost in the movement of Darcy's deft fingers. "If you don't need her, I mean."

"Well, the answer to that question is easy. I'm lonely," she said in a matter-of-fact way whilst cracking two eggs one-handed. "She comes three days a week now, and while she's here, we clean the house together, talk and eat lunch, drink a cocktail or two. And then she goes home to her husband, and I eat dinner alone. She's my best friend. I pay her to be my best friend. Isn't that pathetic?"

"Darcy..." I said softly, slightly stunned at how quickly we'd stumbled into this topic. My assessment of her was never off. She was the sad, pretty housewife. I rounded the island, moved in behind her, and wrapped my arms around her as she tried to hold back her tears.

"Anyway...that's where Minnie is today. Spending time with her family." She twisted in my embrace so she could look me in the eye. "And I'm spending time with you," she whispered before bringing her lips to mine, a soft press and a quick sweep of her tongue before she focused on her task again.

"You know... I was thinking of that conversation we had at lunch the first day I got here."

"What part of it?"

I walked back around to the opposite side of the island and sat on the barstool. I wanted to be able to see her face while we talked. "That bit where you joked about dating a younger man."

Darcy looked up at me, her left eyebrow raised. "You do realize I was just trying to wind Jared up, right?"

"I know, I know, but it got me to thinking," I said, leaning forward on my elbows.

"About what?"

"What would it have been like to meet you in a different way? A different time and place?"

"Different how? Like at some random frat bar when you were in college?" She picked up the whisk and the mixing bowl and began to pace as she mixed the ingredients.

"No," I said, shaking my head. "Not back then, when our age difference was so obvious. I was a kid. You would've never fucked around with me then — regardless of the circumstance."

She stopped mixing the pancakes and turned to me with a look on her face that I couldn't read.

"What?" I asked, worried that I'd said something wrong.

"Nothing. I just... Thank you for saying that because I've been thinking about that and worrying that I might've done or said something to give you the wrong impression back then—"

"No, Darcy. Never—"

"Good. Good... I'm just glad to know that I wasn't inappropriate with you back then."

I had to laugh at that. "Darcy... If you were ever even slightly inappropriate with me back then, last night would have happened a lot sooner because I would have been all in."

Darcy rolled her eyes. "Really, Tommy?" she scolded lightly.

"Yes, really. I've been in love with you for years, and if you'd given me even the slightest..." The words died on my tongue, and I couldn't finish the thought because the look on her face made me realize what I just said. "Shit, I didn't mean to say that."

"Tommy..."

I did love Darcy. Of course, I fucking did. How could I not? But that wasn't her problem. My feelings for her were none of her business.

"Let's just pretend those words never came out of my mouth," I continued, not wanting to hear what her eyes had already told me. "But anyway...what if we met this weekend? You're you now, and I'm me now, and we met at...I don't know... that oyster bar. We're both eating alone at the bar. Would you..." Fuck, now that I'd told her that I love her, this little fantasy felt too vulnerable and not at all fun. "Never mind. This is silly," I said, shaking my head.

"No..." she said. "You want to know what would happen if we met one night while I was eating alone at Leon's...if I would be interested. Of course, I would, Tommy," she said, with a shake of her head and a sad smile. "I would question your interest in me, but yes... I would absolutely be interested."

"Question my interest? Look at you. You have no reason to question why any man would want you, hermosa. I know I would want you just the same. I wouldn't be able to sit at a bar and watch you eat alone without trying to shoot my shot."

She laughed out loud at that. "And I would probably have this exact reaction."

"What could I have done or said to convince you that I was serious?"

Darcy smiled and shrugged again, suddenly shy. "I don't know, Tommy. It's been so long since a man hit on me."

"Come on. That can't be true," I said. "I don't believe that for one second."

"Well, it's true. Outside of lecherous old men, Darcy doesn't get much play."

"So what? You haven't dated at all since your he died?"

"I didn't say that." She ladled three round puddles of pancake batter on the griddle with a thoughtful look on her face. "But, I guess I kinda made them happen, you know?"

"Hm. I do know," I said with a waggle of my brows. "So, in that scenario, you would come on to me. Not the other way around."

"Yeah, probably. But only after I was absolutely sure you were interested."

"So, what would you say? What's your line?"

"I don't have a line."

"You have a line. Everyone has a line, Darcy."

"I really don't." She glanced up at me. "I'd probably compliment your eyes. You have really intense, beautiful eyes, and those dark lashes of yours make them look like they're lined with kohl."

My heart did something weird in my chest, and my cheeks heated. "You really think that?"

"Of course. I've already told you many times that I think you're handsome." She gave me a wink then grabbed a spatula to flip the pancakes. "Would that have worked?"

"I mean...probably. But I liked what you said the other night before you kissed me too."

"And what was that?"

Remembering that night, what she said, and how her expression had changed the moment the words were out of her mouth. "I don't want just any man, Tommy."

"I... I said that?"

"Yup. You said, 'I don't want just any man, Tommy,' and then you mauled me—"

"Mauled you? That's not how I remember it," she said, flipping the pancakes. They were a perfect golden brown, and paired with the sizzling bacon, mingled together to make a mouthwatering scent that made my belly growl again.

"You did. You mauled me, and then jumped into my lap and begged me to touch your pussy—"

"Begged you to... No, sir. You asked to touch my pussy," she corrected, pointing the spatula at me.

I grinned and swiped at it, too slowly to actually grab it, and she slapped it across my knuckles. "Let's just say we both thought it would be a great idea if I touched your pussy."

"I'll concede that." She turned off the heat under the bacon and placed it on a bed of paper towels. "Because it was a good idea."

"Hm," I grunted in the affirmative. "The best idea."

"The best I've had in months. Maybe years," she said with a breathy laugh. "You wanna grab some plates for us?"

"Sure." I stood and went to the set of cabinets behind her to get the plates. "Do you think..." I began slowly. It felt easier to ask this with her back turned. "Do you think if we'd met that way — sitting at the bar at Leon's — do you think we would have had a chance?" I set the plates down next to the stove and stood behind her.

Darcy didn't respond, but she leaned against me, pressing her body against mine. I pressed a soft kiss to the top of her head and breathed her in. I guess she figured that would be answer enough. It wasn't.

16

DARCY

Waking up next to Tommy this morning, I was instantly swept up in a feeling that I was afraid to give a name. Flat on his belly, his legs tangled in the sheets, snoring a little, his back and cute little ass bared to the bright sunlight streaming in through the row of French doors along the piazza, he looked like a dream made real. I'd pressed featherlight kisses down his spine because he was there, and I could. I allowed myself to say and think a word that I had no right to...

Mine.

I wanted Tommy to be mine, and that felt strange to me.

I'd belonged to someone once, but no one had ever been really, truly mine. I've never wanted that with anyone until now, and I couldn't fucking figure out why I wanted him now. I knew I shouldn't waste time on thoughts like that. But that was what I wanted to say when he asked, "Do you think we would have had a chance?" I wanted to say, "Of course, we would have a chance, because I would make you mine, Tommy."

But I didn't say that.

I didn't say anything. I just let him hold me for a while and fed him pancakes instead.

We took our breakfast out on the piazza and ate at the little bistro table. It was the perfect kind of Sunday morning, the kind that made me love my house. Every window and every door was open to catch the breeze off the river. The humidity was down, and the sun played peekaboo behind fluffy white clouds. Tommy had run up to the garçonnière to change into pajama bottoms but remained shirtless per my request. With his hair all sex-mussed and smiling as he ate his pancakes, he looked younger than his thirty-two years, and I felt younger than my fifty-five, and I wondered if I would always feel this way if we were together.

But that was silly. Just sex endorphins. Just chemicals in my brain that already wanted another dose of him. Nothing else. Nothing more than that.

"So, what's waiting for you at home? Marlowe Thompson tied to your bed?" I asked, smiling around the rim of my coffee cup.

Tommy paused mid-bite and gave me a long hard look. "I think you know by now that I like it the other way around."

I squeezed my thighs together, remembering how he'd used his belt to tie his own hands last night.

"Anyway..." he began with a little smirk. "There's actually a ton of work waiting for me at home. I closed on a Gold Coast mansion restoration before I left. It was built in 1888 by the same firm that designed Chicago's Opera House."

"Cobb and Frost?" I asked, my interest piqued.

"Yeah," he said with a grin. "It has all of this detailed wood-work, art glass windows, Santos mahogany hardwood floors... It's going to be a real beauty once we're done, but it's gonna take a lot of work. I'm kinda dreading my inbox right now."

"Maybe I'll get a chance to see it next time I'm in town," I said. As many times as I've been to Chicago to visit Jared, I'd only had lunch a handful of times with both him and Tommy. Now I wondered how I would be in the same zip code without winding up in his bed.

Jesus Christ, what am I doing?

"Yeah," he said, looking down at his half-empty plate. "I would like that," he finished quietly, leaving what needed to be said unsaid.

"You must be really excited," I said after clearing my throat. "Sounds like a dream job."

"Definitely, and it will drum up more interest for my equitable housing foundation, too. The buyer has some influence with the mayor."

I set down my coffee cup, leaned my chin on my hand, and just looked at him. "This is probably going to be weird for me to say right now, considering we've seen each other naked and all, but... I'm so proud of you, Tommy. I'm proud of you and the man you have become."

He bit the corner of his mouth, blushed, and took a moment to gather himself. "Thank you," he said finally.

"I just made it weird, huh?"

He shrugged and gave me one of his boyish grins. "Maybe just a little, but I liked hearing it anyway. I respect you, and what you think of me matters, Darcy. You're a brilliant businesswoman, and you do your job with heart. I only hope that I can live up to that someday."

"Don't be silly, Tommy. I just sell houses and land."

"But you focus on helping people retain their heirs' property too. There's so few people who even know what that is or why it's important to help Black people maintain ownership of their ancestral land." He picked up his napkin and wiped his mouth. "If you're proud of me, I must be doing something right."

I bit my bottom lip to hide the pleased smile that wanted to spread across my face. Compliments tended to make me feel uncomfortable because I so rarely ever heard them from people close to me. But Tommy had always been generous in that way. "Thank you, Tommy," I said quietly.

"Just stating facts," he answered back just as quietly.

"Are you finished eating?" I asked, gesturing at his plate as I began to stand.

"No...sit. Enjoy your coffee. I'll clean up." He stood and began to stack the plates, napkins, and utensils. "Hey," he said softly to get my attention as he leaned over me. I looked up at him, and he gave my lips a soft, sweet kiss.

I smiled against his lips and curled my hand around the back of his neck, prolonging the sweet press of his mouth against mine. Very quickly, it went from sweet to a hungry, but still soft, exploration that I wanted to take further.

"Hm, what are you thinking about, hermosa?"

"Who says I'm thinking about anything besides kissing you?"

"That little growl you just made. You really don't hear yourself when you do that, do you?"

"Nope," I said with a grin. "I didn't even know I made it until you."

"In that case, I'm claiming that as a sound that you only make for me." He gave me another quick kiss, then took our breakfast dishes into the kitchen.

Shifting around the table, I claimed the seat that he'd just emptied to have a better view into the kitchen. I sighed and just drank Tommy in as he got to work tidying up.

He had a sun-browned complexion, and every inch of him was lean and muscled like he spent as much time working out as I did swimming. When he turned and caught me watching him, he offered me a smile and a wink.

"Hermosa," he said with a tsk as if he wasn't enjoying every moment of me watching him.

Damn. Those eyes of his. I wasn't exaggerating when I said I would have complimented him on them if we met at a bar. They were the color of expensive dark rum, mischievous and friendly, and when he looked at me the way he was looking at me right now, intense enough to make me part my thighs.

And I did part them, letting my robe drape open just enough for him to see the place where I wanted him to be.

He bit his lip then glanced at the clock over the kitchen door. A frown creased his brow while he rinsed the dishes, loaded them into the dishwasher, and wiped off the countertops before making his way back out to the piazza.

"Looks like you've arrived a little early for your dick appointment, but I think you might need my attention now." He leaned over me and reached into my robe, fingertips skimming my mound and diving down to glance over my clit.

"I think I do." He tipped my chin upward with his other hand and kissed me. His fingers felt cool against my heated folds.

"You're all wet," he whispered. "What got you this wet, Darcy?"

"Watching you. Watching and loving the way you peacock for me."

He chuckled at that. "What can I say? I love the way you look at me. But I love looking at you more, hermosa." He backed up and held out his hand. "Come here."

I stood and took his hand. He led me over to the more secluded end of the piazza. The same ivy vines that created a dark shelter on the piazza outside of my bedroom created a curtain here where he pulled me down onto the comfortable couch. Just a day ago, I'd lounged on this same couch with my sisters and lamented about the melancholia of old age settling on me now that Jared was married and creating a family of his own. I felt none of that as Tommy pulled me down next to him so we could cuddle together.

With my back to his front, his hold on me felt possessive, and when his big hand spread over my lower belly under my robe, I let myself sink into it because who knew when I would have someone hold me this way again?

Tommy kissed my neck, and his fingers inched toward the apex of my thighs. "Do you want to say it, or should I?" he asked.

"Say what?"

He growled and nipped my neck with the edge of his teeth. It didn't hurt necessarily, but it startled me, and he took that moment to slide his hand down between my legs, holding my pussy in the palm of his hand.

"It's not fair that you're making me be the vulnerable one, hermosa. I know you're thinking it too... I know you're feeling it." He soothed the place he'd nipped with a kiss and a lick, then began to play with my clit with his middle finger while his other hand reached into my robe to pinch my nipples. His touch felt different today. It was tinged with a little anger, and I understood why. This thing that had happened between us over the last few days felt magical. Perfect in some ways, and if I allowed myself to go there, I would use words like *meant to be* and *fate*, but I couldn't keep him, so why give in to those thoughts? Why would I hurt him and myself in that way?

"Saying it won't change anything," I murmured finally.

"I know that. Don't you think I fucking know that?"

His hold on me tightened, his fingers buried deeper inside of me. "Maybe I just want to hear it," he whispered hotly. He withdrew his wet fingertips and painted my clit with my own arousal. "Maybe I just want to hear it. Maybe I just want to hear you say you'll miss me. Miss my touch. That you wish things were different between us. Maybe I just want to hear you say it, hermosa. 'Cause I know, I'll miss you. Miss this."

"Oh, Tommy," I said softly, wanting to give him those words but still afraid of hurting him.

So, I gave him what I could give him in this moment.

Twisting slightly in his embrace, I sought and found his mouth. The moment our lips brushed, he turned their meeting into a needy, desperate kind of thing. His tongue invaded my mouth. My body responded to that invasion and the feel of his hard dick against the crease of my ass, his hips thrusting against me at the same rhythm he made with his tongue. The twin sensations made me so wet that my inner thighs were slippery and refused to stay closed under the careful attentions of his fingers.

"Shit, I'm gonna come," I cursed softly only a second before the pleasure washed over my body, and I immediately wanted more.

I reached back and covered his hardness with my hand. He pressed himself into my palm the moment he felt the contact. Feeling him so hard and so ready and so right there made me reach inside the elastic waistband.

"*Shitttt*...soft, soft, soft, Darcy," he whispered, pressing his lips against my bare shoulder.

He felt so velvety hot in my hand. Thick and weeping at the tip, and I wanted him inside of me just like that. Just the way he felt in my hand.

"Take off your bottoms," I whispered.

He went absolutely still for a moment, and I knew what he was thinking. We were outside and only barely shielded from my neighbors if they chose to get inquisitive. Every door and window in my house was open to the breeze, and if anyone were to come to visit, they could be inside and upon us before we even heard them.

I didn't care.

"Take them off. I want you inside of me. Right now. Just like this," I whispered, stroking my hand up and down his length with a soft, whispering touch.

"But—"

"Just like this," I repeated.

Tommy let out a shaky breath. "You sure?" he asked.

I nodded and tugged at his waistband again until he pulled them off himself, kicking his legs free and sending the pajama bottoms flying. They caught on the little wrought iron chandelier over the bistro table. We both chuckled, and then we kissed, and he untied my robe, exposing my naked body to the soft morning breeze, and all humor left me.

"Open your legs for me, hermosa," he whispered and repositioned us so that our hips aligned. I did as he asked, and that same breeze kissed my drenched sex, and I shivered at the sensation.

"Shhh...I'm right here," he whispered, then I felt the fat, blunt tip of him nestle against my opening. He held still for a long moment, shivering and giving me a look that felt like he could see all of the things I wanted to say and tried to keep buried. He cupped my cheek in his hand, angling my mouth close so he could kiss me as he said, "I'm gonna miss you, hermosa," before thrusting into me, sure and deep and as perfect as his words.

The beginning of a goodbye.

"I'm gonna miss being inside of you, miss feeling you come."

"Please, make me come," I begged.

"Whenever you want, Darcy. Always. I'm yours."

He withdrew and sank in deep again. So deep that my breath caught, stretching and filling me so good that my eyes rolled back in my head. And maybe my memory was just foggy, but it really felt like no one had ever felt this good to me. No one had ever paid such close attention to what made me gasp, moan, and the exact way I played with my clit as he moved his dick *just so,* making sure that every thrust dragged his length against my g-spot.

"Oh, god... I feel you. You're about to come, aren't you? Can I come with you? Can I come inside of you?"

"Yes... I'm..." I couldn't even get the words out before it began to unfurl; slowly at first, then so hard and clenching that I could barely draw a breath.

"Fuck, yes...oh, fuck." Tommy held me tighter and fucked me harder, so hard that it triggered another flutter of pleasure while he held himself still and buried inside of me. I felt every pulse and throb, every hot spurt, as my pussy drew every drop from him.

———

THE NEXT FEW hours moved differently, too fast, yet full of so many flashbulb moments that they seemed to pass in slow motion. Moments I knew I would remember years from now.

Like when he carried me up to my bed, spread me out, and kissed every inch of me as he slid inside of me again, and said, "I can stay an extra day. Maybe more than a day. If I make some calls right now, I can stretch it until the end of the week—"

"No," I said. "It'll just set the hook in deeper and make it harder."

Or when he said, "This feels bigger than I thought it would. Doesn't it feel bigger to you? Like something meant to be?"

"Of course, but it was never meant be more than this. You and me? It can never be anything, Tomás. We knew that at the start."

And when he turned to me in the shower, his eyes cast downward, water droplets on his lashes, and said, "I just want more time, hermosa. Why does it feel like you're saying goodbye forever?"

"It's not forever. We'll see each other again."

"Just not like this," he finished for me, saying the quiet part out loud.

"Not like this."

I rode with him to the airport. I shouldn't have, but letting him leave like that felt too abrupt. I did the same outside of the departure doors. Instead of taking the car home, I got out like we were going away together. The driver even wished us safe travels.

Tommy reached for my hand as we stood next to each other in the check-in line for American Airlines, prolonging the moment when we would actually have to step outside of the fantasy, pop the bubble. In a way, I think I wanted that even less than he did. For the last few days, my house had been full of people and sounds, and liveliness, and him in my bed, and inside of me. On my skin. Worming his way into my heart.

Now, it would be empty again.

After he checked in, we walked hand in hand toward the escalators that led up to the terminals. He turned to me, the muscle in his jaw ticking as he clenched his teeth. "Do you regret it, hermosa?"

"Tommy—"

"I'd be crushed if you did."

"Listen to me," I said, cupping his scruffy cheeks in my palms. "I don't regret one second of it. Not one."

He nodded and took a shuddering breath, then kissed me. Soft, then deep, and for so long that the sounds of travelers, the Muzak, and the garbled announcements from the PA system fell away. He whispered things to me. *Hermosa, hermosa, hermosa*, and other soft words in Spanish until we couldn't prolong the inevitable anymore.

"See you soon, Tomás," I said, then turned and walked away from the only thing I ever wanted to call mine.

17

TOMÁS

"So, I know that traditionally, homes with this much woodwork usually have a darker stain throughout. But I wanted you to see some of the options before we settle on the same ol' boring thing we always do," Juana, my little sister and interior decorator, said.

We were standing in front of a recently renovated home in Bronzeville. Back in the day, Bronzeville was known as the Black Metropolis and had the nation's most significant concentration of Black businesses. Thousands of Black Americans had escaped the oppression of the South by migrating to Chicago in search of industrial jobs. Today, it was one of the areas in the city most affected by gentrification. The difference, in this case, was that these homes were mostly bought and renovated by affluent Blacks. It didn't really matter who purchased the homes; the effect was still the same — low and middle-income families were priced out of the homes and neighborhoods they'd lived in for generations. I was currently in negotiations with the city to buy up a few empty lots to build some mixed-income housing, but there'd been a bit of pushback from the newer, more affluent residents.

A lot of pushback, actually.

"How did you find out about this place?" I asked, pinning Juana with a disparaging look.

She rolled her eyes. "Our realtor. I simply asked her if she'd come across some renos with the kind of detailed woodwork in the Cobb & Frost mansion, and she sent me some links. I dug through them until I found one with the kinda stain I think we should use on that job. Just...come inside and keep an open mind."

"Fine," I said with a heavy sigh and followed her up the steps and onto the porch.

Progress on the Cobb & Frost house was humming along. Not a hitch in the plans so far. It had been almost unnervingly easy. There was already lots of interest from buyers as well, and it looked like I would make back my money threefold.

Everything was going great, but I was finding it hard to give a fuck.

This was my dream job, all the exposure I wanted for my firm, but it felt...anticlimactic. I just kept thinking, I finish this job, and then, what? I just look for the next one? And the next, and the next, until I was an old, rich man that people paid fifteen hundred dollars a plate just to be in the same room with, in hopes that they might rub elbows with me? *Is this all there is?*

I shook my head and focused my attention on the home that I was about to enter. It was a Romanesque townhouse, three levels, with a deep porch and two front doors. "Splitting them into apartments?" I asked as Juana fumbled with the key holder.

"Yeah, two one-bedroom, 1 1/2 baths, and a studio in the attic. Damn it. My nails are too long. I can't get this thing open."

"Here," I said, tapping her on the shoulder and gesturing for her to step aside. "What's the combo?" She recited it to me, and I spun the dials, and the box popped open. As I opened the doors, I did the math on what the buyer was looking to net on this purchase and realized pretty quickly that some of the older apartment homes on this block and the next would eventually raise their rents to draw in the types that would rent this high-end product.

Shit.

And whoever bought this place probably thought they were doing a good thing. That the neighborhood would benefit from these positive changes. Some folks who bought into this particular American Dream were just ignorant to how it would affect the demographic makeup of the neighborhood and disrupt the culture that made them want to live here in the first place. Others didn't care. Still, others felt that it was inevitable and unstoppable, so why shouldn't they get a piece of the pie if it was gonna happen anyway? These were the people I was up against, and suddenly, it all felt pointless.

"See? It has just as much wainscoting and heavy crown molding as the Gold Coast mansion, but in this lighter stain, it feels, well, lighter. I feel like it opens the space up."

I nodded. "How does it measure up comp-wise? Are there homes like the Gold Coast mansion on your list with this light finish?"

"Well...no, but—"

"So, it doesn't make sense to use finishes or make stylistic choices that won't appeal to the target buyer for this product." I looked around, ran my fingers along the silken, high-gloss, damn near honey-colored stain. "It's beautiful, but if we chose this, and it affected the bottom line—"

Juana turned to me with her hands on her hips. "So negative before you even run the numbers? What is going on with you, Tomás? Your attitude is for shit these days."

Stunned by her outburst, I stepped back and crossed my arms. "I wasn't aware that I had anything going on but this job. You seem to think otherwise."

She sighed. "I'm just saying that you seem different lately. You don't seem as excited as you were when you signed the paperwork for this house. Did something happen that I should know about?"

Laughing, I shook my head. "Nothing is going on, Juana. I just want to make sure we're making sound business decisions." I shrugged and walked the perimeter of the room. "But I was dismissive with you just now, so I apologize for that."

"Thank you," she said in a small voice.

"This is a big job for both of us. Could push us into an entirely different market, so if it feels like I'm playing it safe, that's why. I still don't believe a lighter stain would appeal to our prospective buyers, but find me some comps at that price point, and we'll revisit this in a few days."

A bright smile split her face, and my little sister was damn cute when she got her way. "I've got some great ideas, hermano. I know that these rich academic types like that dark masculine look, but we can start new trends, you know?" she rambled as she followed me back toward the door.

I stood at the top of the front steps and looked out at the neighborhood as my sister continued to chatter on behind me. It wasn't quite fall yet, but I could already see that the leaves on the trees that lined this quiet street were beginning to yellow. The air had that crisp bite, a warning that a Chicago winter was definitely coming, and if you wanted to get out, now was the time.

I had lots of thoughts about getting out lately.

I wanted to sell all of my shit — including my company — and book a ticket to Charleston. Drive straight to that Victorian Charleston single crowded with lush greenery two blocks from the Ashley River. Find the cat-eyed woman who owned it, the same woman who'd stolen my heart fifteen years ago, and beg her to keep me forever.

Juana wasn't wrong. My head couldn't be further out of the

game than it had been since I came back from Charleston. But that was how I felt every time I came home from there, wasn't it? Like all of it was some hot, sticky, drunken fever dream that happened outside of reality. This trip felt even more other-worldly because I'd sacrificed myself to a benevolent goddess who devoured me only to spit me out.

Sigh.

That wasn't fair to her.

I knew what it was before she led me up to her bedroom. We both did. But like a child, I'd gone in overeager and expecting a different outcome. It wasn't her fault that she was better at accepting reality than I was.

"So, where are you headed?" Juana asked. "We could get some drinks before dinner."

"I won't be at dinner tonight. Jared and Brandi invited me over to their new place."

My little sister came to stand next to me. "I still can't believe someone married his arrogant ass."

"Brandi is actually perfect for him. You'd be surprised," I said with a raised brow.

"If you say so," she grumbled.

My little sister had had a crush on Jared since the first day she set her big brown eyes on him. Anyone could see it, but she tried to hide it by being mean and confrontational whenever he was around. Jared would never go there, though. Juana was too young.

Too young. Hm. What right did I have to make that determination when I'd been sniffing around Darcy since I was much younger than my sister was now?

"So, where'd they buy their house?" Juana asked as we descended the stairs to our respective cars.

"They bought a place in Streeterville on N. Water Street.

Low-rise, new build, which isn't great, but it's close to the hospital and has room enough for them to start a family."

"Wow. Streeterville."

I shrugged. "This'll be my first time visiting. You know how I feel about new construction going up near the waterfront, but what can you do?"

"What can you do?" she echoed. Juana turned to me and gave me a hug. "Are you're sure you're okay?"

"I'm fine," I said, hugging her back.

Her hold around my neck tightened. "You know you can talk to me, right?"

For a moment, I considered telling her, but what would I say? *I'm in love with my best friend's mother. Tell me a way we can be together without ruining our relationships with her son.*

Pushing her away, I gave her a quick kiss on the cheek. "Quit worrying. I'm fine. Tell mama I love her," I called over my shoulder before hopping into my pickup truck and pointing it toward Jared and Brandi's place.

Traffic was slow, which gave me more time to obsess over the fact that I hadn't heard from Darcy since I left Charleston. We never said that we would text or call, and it was probably best that we didn't. But we still shared a calendar, and occasionally — and by occasionally, I mean daily — I checked her schedule to see what she was doing.

Today at four p.m., she had lunch with the Dalys. The Dalys were prospective clients looking for a home in Wagner Terrace. It was a hip little neighborhood with a lot of ranch-style homes a few minutes north of where Darcy lived in South Broad. She was taking them to The Butcher & The Bee, where we'd eaten lunch my first day in Charleston. Later, she had to stop by the bank and her lawyer's office.

Yes, this was more than obsessive and bordered on stalker-ish, but if I couldn't be with her, what harm was it to imagine her

as she made her way through her day? Or to take it a step
further and imagine myself waiting for her in that Charleston
single, all the windows and doors thrown wide to let in the crisp
autumn evening air, and that big copper soaking tub filled with
her favorite bath salts and oils, just waiting to soothe her work-
weary body?

It had been damn near five months, but I was still struggling to settle back into my normal, everyday life. I mean, shit.
Did I even believe normal life was possible anymore? Everything felt too harsh, too sharp, razor-edged since I'd been
home. Life, before I made love to Darcy, was only occasionally
interrupted by brief bouts of daydreaming about her. Life after
making love to her wasn't a daydream anymore. I knew her
taste. Knew the tone and vibrato of each of her moans. Knew
how her pussy gripped my dick when she was close to coming.
All of this, in addition to the things I already knew and loved
about her? This knowledge of Darcy MacFarland was going to
be my undoing.

I was never more certain of that than when Jared swung
open the door to welcome me into his new home.

How fucking twisted was it that when I looked at my best
friend, I saw the shape of his mother's eyes and the slope of her
nose? Because I did, and it made me miss her even more.

"Finally!" Jared bellowed, stretching his arms wide.

I laughed at my friend as I stepped across the threshold and
accepted his hug. Jared thumped me on the back and dragged
me further into the front hall of his home.

"Calm down, bro. It hasn't been that long," I said, pushing
him away with an awkward laugh.

"Are you serious right now? I've only seen you like a handful
of times since the wedding."

"Because I wanted to give the newlyweds room to settle into
married life."

Jared pulled a face and narrowed his eyes at me. "Bullshit. You've been avoiding me."

I froze. Guilt rendered me stiff while I grasped for an explanation. Did he know why I was avoiding him? Did he suspect that it had something to do with Darcy? No. He couldn't. If he knew, he would have confronted me... Unless this was the confrontation. Had my best friend of almost fifteen years invited me to dinner, a few beers, and an ass whooping for fucking his mother?

Jared leveled an unreadable look at me. That was even more disconcerting. It was bizarre to see my long-time friend make a face I'd never seen before. Was this his murder face?

"Listen," he said, dropping a hand on my shoulder and giving it a rough squeeze. "I get it. I'm married now, and you're a perpetual bachelor. Maybe you think we have nothing in common anymore. Or maybe you're worried monogamy is contagious or that our relationship is going to change. Whatever the case, I get it. You needed some time."

It took me a minute, but eventually, the joke set in, and I laughed. "I'm not at all worried about monogamy being contagious," I answered truthfully because how could I be? The one woman I wanted to spend the rest of my life with was the one person I couldn't have, and fuck! *I need to let this gooooo...*

"Whatever," Jared rolled his eyes. "Hang up your coat. I'll get you a beer. Brandi is running late."

I shrugged out of my jacket and hung it on the row of hooks near the front door. "Is she on call? I thought she had the night off."

"She does, but the on-call who was supposed to relieve her was running late...whatever. She'll explain it when she gets here. But don't make it a big deal, okay? She's doing this thing where she's trying to be the perfect wife." He made air quotes around those two words and rolled his eyes again. "I keep telling her that we're both doctors, and it's super unrealistic to expect either of us to have some sort of nine-to-five lifestyle where we eat dinner together every night, but she's dead set on it..."

I shook my head and laughed. Now we were back in familiar territory. Jared Territory.

We took our beers on a tour of Jared's new two-story, three-bedroom, three-bath townhome. It was builder basic — high-end finish builder basic, but basic none the less. Stark white walls, bland blond engineered wood floors, pressed wood crown molding, kitchen and bathroom packages from Lowes or Home Depot, with hard surface countertops and bronzed fixtures. I hated it. But I could tell that Jared wanted my approval, so I made all of the appropriate sounds and thumped him on the back. At least Brandi had done a good job decorating it.

"This is a beautiful home you've made for you and your little wife. I'm proud of you."

"Really?"

"Absolutely. You really did good."

"Thanks. Let's go out back and light up the fire pit—"

"I'm here! I'm here! I'm here!" Brandi called out frantically as she burst through the front door, her arms full of grocery bags. "I'm so sorry I'm late. I had a last-minute aneurysm roll in, and the on-call neurosurgeon wasn't answering his phone, and—"

"It's okay, baby. It's okay," Jared said. He went to her, kissed her, and took the bags out of her hands. "Me and Tomás are perfectly capable of entertaining ourselves."

"I know, but it's already so late and—"

"Baby..." Jared pulled her into his arms, whispered something to her, and kissed her again. Brandi smiled and softened in his arms.

I turned my back to give them some privacy. It was a private moment. Yup. That was exactly why I couldn't watch my friend soothe his cute, frazzled wife. I wasn't jealous or anything. Not at all. Not even a little bit.

I guzzled down what was left of my beer.

"Hey, Tommy!" Brandi called out. Before I could turn around, I found Brandi's arms around me, giving me one of her firm bear hugs. "So glad you finally came over. I'm making salmon. You like salmon, right?

"Love it," I said, turning to face her.

She smiled, and now I understood why Jared had asked me to go with the flow. Brandi was clearly stretching herself thin, but when she gave me that big smile, Jared smiled too. I knew how it felt to want to make your woman's load lighter, to make her smile.

Who's making Darcy smile now?

Dinner was late, and by the time Brandi served the overcooked but well-seasoned salmon, I was halfway in the bag and ravenous enough to eat more than one helping without complaint.

The three of us cleaned the kitchen together, and then Jared and I took the last of the beers onto the back patio.

"Brandi's not gonna join us?" I asked.

Jared glanced at me with a smirk on his face, and I knew why. Even I could hear how slurred my words were.

Beer drunk on a Thursday night. Bueno.

"Nah," Jared said finally as he lit the fire pit. "She has the early shift again tomorrow."

"Well, shit," I said, preparing to stand. "I should go. You probably want to fuck your wife."

"Relax, vaquero," Jared said, slamming a big hand into the middle of my chest and forcing me back down into my chair. "You need to sober up a bit, then Uber home."

I sank back into the patio chair. "Good call," I said, kicking my feet up on the rim of the stone fire pit. "I mean...why the fuck am I rushing home anyway? Ain't nobody there waitin' for me." I tipped up my beer bottle with a wry chuckle.

"Never knew that being alone was a problem for you."

"Didn't used to be," I murmured under my breath.

Jared twisted in his chair and gave me a pointed look.

"What?" I asked when he'd stared at me for an awkwardly long time without saying anything.

"Are you trying to tell me something? Is there some girl you're seeing that I don't know about?"

"What? Nah...nah...there's no girl. But I'm not that thing you called me by the door earlier."

"What? A perpetual bachelor?"

"Yeah. I mean, I don't know what would give you that impression, but—"

"Are you fucking kidding me? The weather girl was your last long-term relationship, and that was over a year ago. Since then, you haven't been interested in dating. You won't let Brandi hook you up with any of her friends—"

"I can't date a fucking doctor. Y'all keep ridiculous schedules. I might as well stay single."

"Not all of her friends are doctors, Tomás. But you haven't taken her up on it, so how would you know?" Jared shook his head. "Pffttt...you want to be alone."

"Maybe. But that still doesn't mean I want to be alone forever—"

"You're not interested in dating or relationships, Tommy? How the fuck do you think that's supposed to turn out?"

How the fuck was that supposed to turn out? There was an answer to his question, but I was sure it wasn't one he wanted to hear or that I could ever tell him. Darcy had occupied that space in my heart long before I ever thought of filling it. Now that I'd been with her, it was hard to even think of anyone else in that way.

It was ridiculous. I *knew* it was. But I couldn't deny that I'd constantly compared the women I dated to her over the years. She was intelligent, soulful, caring, kind, and so fucking beautiful. So unbelievably sexy and beautiful that I could barely look at her sometimes, but even with all that, she was a down-to-earth country girl. Ambitious enough to be successful all on her own while caring deeply for her family and friends.

Darcy was the blueprint for me, but I couldn't fucking have her. I needed some time to get over that.

"I..." I paused to clear my throat because my voice was too thick with emotion. "I remain hopeful that I will find someone who makes me as happy as Brandi has made you someday. But for right now—"

"Yeah, I know. You're focused on your business," Jared finished for me, his tone short and clipped.

"Hey, what's with all this bullshit? Are you angry with me or something?"

"To be honest, yes. I just thought we would be going through these stages together."

I frowned. "What do you mean?"

"You know...getting married, having kids, watching the game on the big screen on the weekends while our kids play in the fucking yard, and our wives drink wine in the kitchen and talk shit about us."

"Why are they talking shit about us?"

"I don't fucking know, Tommy. Maybe I'm not fucking my wife enough, and you have a honey-do list that's as long as your ass is tall. Fuck if I know. It's what married couples do. They complain about each other, then go home and fuck anyway because that's what love is."

"Oh-kay, I'm drunk, but how does that make sense? And are you not fucking Brandi enough?"

"She may have complained about it a few times, but that's

not the fucking point, Tomás. We were supposed to be going through these stages together. I can't talk to you about married life because your ass ain't married."

"I mean... I get it. I thought I would be too."

But was that true?

How could I think that we would ever be able to go through those stages together when Darcy was the only woman I'd ever truly wanted?

"Maybe I just need to get out more. Not work so much," I conceded.

"Definitely that," Jared readily agreed. "Maybe take a vacation or something."

"I just took a vacation when you got married—"

"That wasn't a vacation. That was four days of being my best man and taking care of my mother. I mean a real vacation. Two weeks or a month somewhere warm. Isn't that supposed to be a perk of being a business owner?"

"I heard that somewhere...yeah," I agreed.

"Well, you need to do it. You've hired three architects in the past year. You can delegate and take some time for yourself before you burn the fuck out. Because that's where this is headed."

Jared wasn't wrong. I did need to get out of Chicago and out of my own fucking head.

I STUMBLED out of my Uber and rode the elevator up to my condo. Had this building always felt this cold and sterile to me? Admittedly, I should live in some renovated townhome like the one I saw in Bronzeville today, but I thought it seemed too much like a place a man looking for a wife would buy.

Haha. Joke's on me.

Amazing how getting the one thing I've always wanted more

than anything made all of my previous accomplishments feel pointless and empty. I'd never really understood that statement until I opened the door to my condo.

Sweeping city views greeted me. My cleaning lady came by this afternoon, so everything smelled faintly of bleach and purple Fabuloso. Everything was neat, clean, and undisturbed.

It felt and looked like a fucking tomb.

"Fuck this," I cursed out loud in the empty apartment. Stripping out of my clothes and leaving them in the middle of the floor, I poured myself some more whiskey and opened my laptop.

It was time to plan my fucking escape.

18

DARCY

"Darcy Anne MacFarland!" Minerva exclaimed as she stormed into my bedroom.

I groaned and rolled onto my side. "I could've sworn I told you that I didn't need you today."

"Hm. As if I didn't see right through that lie." She stalked across the room and yanked open the heavy blackout curtains I always installed when the weather turned cold. A flood of pale, wintery sunlight flooded the room. "Look at all of this dust!"

"Minerva, please," I grumbled.

"Please, nothing. I haven't been here in almost three weeks. And I said to myself that there's only two reasons why you wouldn't want me to come over. You either hired someone else, or you're over here rolling in your own filth." Minerva came to stand over me. "And here I find you in bed at midday."

"Yeah, well, I don't feel great."

"I reckon you don't with all of that whiskey you've been drinking. I saw the bottles in the trash before I emptied it. Had the whole house stinking like Bourbon Street on a Friday night during Mardi Gras."

"Okay, whatever. Will you close the blinds so I can sleep off this hangover?"

"No, ma'am. You've done enough of that. Time to get out of this bed and into the bath."

I opened my eyes and glared at her. "Last time I checked, my mama was Black and living on Daniel Island."

Minerva narrowed her eyes until they were nothing but glittering, blue shards. "You're right about that. Would you like me to get her on the phone so she can come down here and drag her daughter out of bed?"

"Are you seriously threatening to call my mother?"

"You're the one who brought her up! If getting her on the phone will get you out of these stale sheets and into the shower to put some hot water and soap on your body, I'll do it." She folded her arms over her chest and shifted her weight onto one foot. "So, what's it gonna be? Should I go start the shower?"

Defeated, I sighed and closed my eyes. "Fine."

"Good." Minerva turned her back and marched into my bedroom. "I'll lay some fresh pajamas out for you too."

"I'm not saying thank you!" I yelled at her back.

Irritated, I kicked off the covers in a small, silent tantrum. So what, it was midday on Tuesday, and I'd been drinking since Sunday night? Work was slow, and I had no kids to take care of — not to mention the fact that I was fifty-five goddamn years old. I'd earned this wallow. I was allowed.

But had it really been three weeks since Minnie had come by to clean the house?

Well, yeah...that sounds about right.

Because three weeks ago, Tommy had added his trip to Costa Rica to our shared calendar. At first, I thought it was an invitation. I mean, sure, we hadn't communicated since he left in June, but my heart had damn near broken free of my chest when I saw it. I immediately took a screenshot of the event and sent him a playful, "are you trying to tell me something?" text. He responded within seconds with an apology. Said he was drunk. That he'd put it on our shared calendar by accident, and wow. That had hurt more than it fucking should have.

But still hopeful and glad to be texting him again, I had tried to keep the communication flowing.

ME: Costa Rica, huh?

TOMMY: Yeah. Jared told me that
I needed to take a vacation
because I was showing
all the textbook signs of burnout.
He was right.
So I decided to get the fuck
out of here for a while.

ME: How long is a while though?
No return flight?

TOMMY: I don't know yet. I took a month,
but maybe it'll end up being more than that.

ME: What about Son of Martin?
And all of the work you've done on
your equitable housing initiatives?

TOMMY: I recently hired three architects.
One of them, Lauryn, is more connected than
I am when it comes to the dealing with our
equitable housing projects so
she'll be handling it while I'm gone.
The Cobb & Frost job is almost done.

I don't need to be here for it run smoothly.
Besides, it's a five-hour flight.
I can always fly home if there's an emergency.

This was all stuff I knew. I'd watched his company grow via social media over the last six months. Watched him hire those three architects, one of whom was a long-legged, dark-skinned beauty named Lauryn, who seemed everpresent in both his personal and business feeds lately. I saw them leave the Craftsman bungalow they'd worked out of for the last four years and move into a larger, more corporate office. I'd watched it all happen. I'd even liked a few of those posts and praised him a bit. Now I was beginning to realize that this was probably growth he'd planned just so he could take this extended trip. To relocate to Costa Rica and never come back.

Then, like a fool, I'd told him that I missed him. His answering text was full of so much venom that my fingertips had stung from it.

TOMMY: *What the fuck do you expect*
me to do with that, Darcy?

He'd apologized. I apologized, and then he apologized some more, but three weeks later, those words were still dogging my thoughts.

What the fuck do you expect me to do with that, Darcy?
What, indeed.

I took a shower and dressed myself in clean pajamas. By the time I made it down to the kitchen, the smell of my favorite breakfast foods filled the air — even though it was no longer breakfast time. Hell, it was even too late for brunch. I shuffled into the room sheepishly and sat at the breakfast bar.

"Coffee?" Minerva asked.

"Yes, please."

Guilt swamped me as she poured my coffee into my favorite mug, made just the way I liked. "I'm sorry," I said when she set the cup in front of me. "I didn't mean to snap at you upstairs. I'm just—"

"Feeling blue. I know. I was here the last time. Remember?"

I nodded and sipped my coffee, feeling appropriately chastised. Because Minerva was here, the last time I spiraled like this. She was there after every miscarriage. After the cancer diagnosis and the hysterectomy. In truth, Minerva was better equipped to handle this than anyone who knew me.

"So..." she began while spooning grits, eggs, and bacon on a plate with two mile high biscuits. "Are you ready to tell me what's got you down this time?"

I shook my head, unwilling to unload this particular sin. "I don't know that it's one thing," I answered vaguely.

"Hm," she said, handing me the plate. "You've been like this since Jared announced his engagement. I thought it would let up after the wedding. Especially since you seemed to be in such good spirits during the festivities." Minerva leaned against the counter and regarded me with raised eyebrows.

"It's a big milestone. Like empty nest times a thousand. I'm allowed to have a hard time with this."

"That's absolutely true. You are. But you've seemed a bit worse the last couple of weeks. Did something happen?"

I tried to ignore it. Tried to bury it under the mouthful of grits, eggs, and a bite of bacon. But the tears welling in my eyes and the tightening in my throat made it too hard to swallow. I stared at my plate and kept chewing as I blinked the tears back.

"You can tell me," she said softly. "You know you can tell me anything."

And I could. She knew everything about me, so why not this? "I did something I shouldn't have," I sputtered.

The whole story poured out of me. Every bit, from start to finish. The proposition. The kiss on the wrist. The brush of lips by the pool. Watching him in the shower. The night on my piazza...the eighteen hours we spent together. I told her everything. Every feeling and every thought that passed through my head during the time we spent together. Every feeling and thought I'd had since. Told her about our shared calendar, and the trip to Costa Rica, and the harsh words he had for me a few weeks ago. I told her all of this, but I didn't even say his name.

I didn't have to.

"I knew that mannish boy was nothing but trouble."

"But he wasn't, Minnie. He woke me up, and... I think... I think I might..." I couldn't say the words out loud, but that didn't matter either.

Minnie nodded knowingly. "I know. I know."

She sighed and let her head sag between her shoulders. She held that position for a long moment, then turned, opened the freezer, and pulled out the half-empty bottle of whiskey. Grabbing a mug from the cabinet, she poured herself some coffee and sweetened it with a generous pour.

I ate, and she drank, and when both my plate and her mug were empty, she set her piercing blue eyes on me.

"So, what do you want, Darcy? What do you want to do about this?"

"What do you mean?"

"I mean, you think you might be in love with this boy, and he's always been in love with you, so what do you want? What are you going to do about it?"

"He's my son's best friend, Minnie. His *very* best friend! It doesn't matter what I want. There's nothing to do."

"Of course, there is."

"No, there isn't. We can't be together."

"And why? Why can't you be together? What are you afraid of?"

"Uh... I could destroy my relationship with my only son, and he'd could lose his best friend for something that might only be a fling."

"So, don't tell him. Don't tell Jared."

"Minerva!"

"What? It's not like it's something you haven't already done."

I stared at her in disbelief. Was she drunk already? "But that was just one night. I can't do that to Tommy. He deserves better than to be treated like some dirty secret."

"Have you asked him about this?"

"Why would I? It's not like I can—"

"Again, why not? If you take the time to figure out if this thing between the two of you is real before you bring it to Jared, I can't see him denying you or Tommy happiness."

I shook my head. I couldn't do that. I couldn't ask Tommy to do that. He deserved to be loved out loud.

"No, that's not an option. Besides, he basically told me he was going to Costa Rica to get over this thing."

"Hm." Minerva reached for the whiskey bottle again, but she didn't bother with the coffee this time as she poured some in each of our mugs. "Costa Rica...is a long way away from everything and everyone he knows." Her eyes met mine over the rim of her mug as she brought it to her lips. "And everyone you know, too," she added.

"It is, I guess..." My mug was halfway to my mouth before I realized what she was saying. The suggestion that she'd left unsaid. It was far away from everything and everyone we knew. If I went with him, I could love him out loud. We could test the waters to see if what we felt for each other had a future.

His caustic words came back to me as I took a sip of the whiskey.

What the fuck do you expect me to do with that, Darcy?
The question was if he would even want me to join him.

————

IT HAD BEEN a long time since I'd been to The Cocktail Bar. Shannon had always liked it more than I did. And as it turned out, he brought Jolene here when I wasn't around so I felt it was best to meet her at the place she felt most comfortable to deliver my news. Not that finally agreeing to sell my real estate business and give her a share of the profits was bad news. She'd wanted me to sell when we were settling Shannon's estate, but I wasn't ready to do it then. But now I was about to blow my life up, and I needed the money from the sale to finance it.

Blowing up my life...

I had to stop thinking of it that way. Starting over in your fifties was completely normal. There were plenty of women who reinvented themselves and launched successful second careers at my age. Except I wasn't selling my business to start something new. I was just chasing a man to Costa Rica. A man that I wasn't even brave enough to call and share that plan with.

I was wrong before. *This* was how you lost your mind.

Jolene was late, per usual, so I ordered a drink and sipped it until she came through the door. As she searched the room, I caught a glimpse of what Shannon probably saw in her when they first met. She couldn't have always been this desperate version of herself, grasping at the scraps and edges of someone else's life.

"Darcy," she said as she pulled out her chair and sat. We were alone, so she didn't bother to perform her good graces or place the usual perfunctory kiss on my cheek.

"Jolene," I said, returning her greeting as I signaled to the waiter. "I ordered you a drink."

"Thanks," she said, accepting the drink with a wary frown on her brow. "So why did you want me to meet you here? What's this about?"

"I've found a buyer for MacFarland Brokerage."

The furrow in Jolene's brow deepened which was a feat considering the amount of money she spent on botox. "A buyer? I wasn't aware that you were selling. I thought you said—"

"I know what I said, but...circumstances have changed." I looked down into my glass. "I have changed," I added.

"I see." She picked up her glass and swirled the brown liquid, making the ice tinkle a bit. "I'm a bit surprised. You were totally against it when we were in probate."

"That was when the business was still new, and it was my only source of income. That's not the case anymore. Like I said, my circumstances have changed, and—"

"You've changed," she interrupted before I could repeat myself. "I heard you the first time. But if I know one thing about you, Darcy MacFarland, it's that you hate change. What inspired this? Have you met someone?"

I smirked and picked up my glass. "It doesn't matter what inspired it, but I'm ready to sever our ties. I thought this would be great news for you. You so wanted to have things completely severed in the past."

"Hm," she grunted. "Well... I hate to break it to you, but we'll never be completely severed. Your son and my son are family."

"I know," I said with a nod. "Jared is starting his own family now, and I think it's time for me to be a bit selfish. I've always envied that."

"Envied what?"

"Your selfishness. You've always gone after anything and anyone you wanted with little regard for consequences. I've always wished I could be that selfish. I guess now is as good a time as any to start." Thinking about what she just said, something occurred to me that I'd never considered before. I shifted in my seat and leaned forward, bracing my elbows on the table. "You know... I don't know much about you, Jolene. We met under the worst circumstances so there is little chance that we will ever be besties who brunch together on Sunday's after church."

The younger woman rolled her eyes. "You're right about that."

I smiled. "But just now... I realized that you're not the villain I made you out to be."

"Oh, really? What changed your mind?"

"What you just said about our sons. You want a family for Dylan."

The corners of her mouth wobbled a bit. "I think that's what every mother wants, isn't it?"

"It is," I agreed with a nod. "Which is why I'm done hating you, Jojo. You loved Shannon, too. He lied to you, too. You lost him, too. We're no different." I reached into my bag, pulled out the purchase agreement, and set it on the table. "Everything is all laid out for you. If you have any questions or problems, I need you to let me know before the end of the week."

"Before the end of the week?" she echoed incredulously. "Today is Wednesday. I need more time to look this over—"

"By Friday close of business, Jolene," I said, standing up from the table. "I need that signed by Friday close of business."

"Darcy... I don't understand. What's the rush? Why can't I get this back to you next week?"

I picked up my glass and drank the last of my cocktail. "I will be out of the country next week."

"Out of the country?" she parroted. "For how long?"

I shrugged and gave her a smile. "Hopefully, indefinitely."

19

TOMÁS

W arm, inviting light shone from the windows of Jared and Brandi's home as I rang the doorbell. Standing on their stoop, I considered that by this time tomorrow, I would be in Costa Rica. Everything was planned. The tickets had been purchased, the villa reserved, my bags were packed. Everything was set up to keep Son of Martin running smoothly while I was gone. Tropical heat, palm trees, and La Pura Vida awaited me. Still, the thought of leaving had my stomach in knots. I hadn't figured out why. It wasn't as if this was the first time I'd ever left home or traveled abroad. The trip had no end date, but it wasn't as if I was never coming back. My friends and family would be here when I figured things out. But for some reason, I couldn't shake the feeling that this decision had some gravity or finality to it. No matter how hard I tried, I couldn't shake that feeling, and it made me reluctant to leave. Regardless, Brandi had decided that this Friendsgiving dinner would also be a going-away party for me.

Friendsgiving.

I was still trying to decide if that was a label you assigned to a group of misfits and strays that didn't have anywhere to go for the holidays. Normally I ate with my family — a dinner full of nontraditional Thanksgiving fare — then I went to the bar to watch the game with my brother. But this year, Jared and Brandi were hosting. A first since he usually spent the holidays in Charleston with Darcy. What was she doing for the holidays without him there? Probably spending it with her parents and the rest of her extended family. The pictures I saw on her Instagram timeline earlier this month implied that much, but I'd also noticed that she looked a little tense and sad in those photos.

Any excuse to obsess over her.

I recognized it for what it was, though. The sort of obsession a kid would have over his hot English teacher. My first crush had been hard to shake, and this thing with Darcy was no different. If I allowed myself to talk about her every time she crossed my mind, Jared would know how I felt about her even if I never said the actual words. Holding that back from him put a strain on our friendship, so I knew that it didn't matter if I was ready to leave. It was time to go.

"Hey!" Brandi exclaimed, offering a big smile as she opened the door wearing a sweater with a turkey appliquéd across the front.

I laughed. "Hey, Bran. I came bearing gifts."

"What? I told you not to bring anything! We have everything covered."

"Are you sure? Because I can absolutely take my mom's tamales home and polish them off myself before getting on the plane in the morning."

"Hold on now. Your mother's tamales? Let's not be hasty. These tamales are apparently legendary, according to Jared." She confiscated the Tupperware dish full of the tamales my mother and sister had made to ensure that I didn't show up empty-handed. "Come in! You're the last one here, and there's someone I want you to meet."

I shrugged off my coat and hung it on the overloaded coat tree in the entryway, then followed her into the family room. Whoever she wanted me to meet was definitely someone she'd been trying to hook me up with for a while. I didn't really see the point since I was leaving tomorrow, but hey, maybe I would be interested enough to knock the dust off before I hopped on the plane. I still felt like a stud on parade when I entered the room behind her.

"Caitlin, Tomika, this is Jared's friend Tomás."

"Heyyy..." I said awkwardly, giving the girls an awkward wave.

Caitlin was a petite blonde with big, blue eyes and a pair of lips on her that could easily inspire some filthy thoughts if you were inclined to do so. "Hi," she said, thrusting out her hand with an eager bounce.

Cute. Too young, but cute. "Nice to meet you, Caitlin."

"Excuse me if I don't get up. I just finished an eighteen-hour shift," Tomika said from her spot on the couch.

Hm. Tomika looked like my type. Dark-skinned with a close-cropped haircut on a head that would fit easily in the palm of my hand. Her brown eyes did look tired, though, and she seemed very comfortable, reclined as she was in the corner of the couch.

"I'll come to you then." I walked around the coffee table, and she sat up slowly like a queen who had been disturbed while in repose. A smirk twitched the corner of her mouth upward as she presented her hand.

"Nice to finally meet you." Her voice had a rich depth to it that reminded me a bit of Darcy's — minus the Southern accent, of course.

Jesus... Can I make it more than ten minutes without thinking of her?

"So you're the one Brandi wanted me to meet," I said,

attempting to flirt with her. I wasn't failing at it, but I was a little rusty.

"I am indeed. We would have met a lot sooner, but you have some sort of issue with doctors."

"Not an issue with doctors, per se—"

"You do have an issue with doctors," Brandi cosigned.

"How dare you imply that I'm prejudice against doctors? Some of my best friends are doctors!" I exclaimed, which drew a cackle from redolent Queen on the couch.

"Yeah, right..." Brandi said as she made her way to the kitchen.

"As I was saying, I don't have an issue with doctors. You just work crazy hours. Seems like you all don't have time to date people who aren't in the same profession."

Tomika's smirk stretched into a smile as she sank back onto the couch cushions. "We do work crazy hours, which means we have to get creative. Are you creative, Tomás?" she asked. Her gaze took a trip down the length of my body that woke up something in me that had been sleeping for the last few months. I didn't know if it was enough to act on, but I was definitely curious.

"I've been accused of being creative in the past," I answered finally.

The sliding glass door to the patio slid open. "Aye!" Jared bellowed. "Good! You're here. You can come help me with this fried turkey."

The fire pit was roaring out back, and Jared thrust a beer into my hand the moment I stepped outside. A few more of his doctor friends that I'd met at one time or another were huddled around the fire, but he pulled me away from them after I said my hellos. He'd been strange about the news of my trip to Costa Rica, even though he was the one who suggested it. Maybe he hadn't anticipated that I would be gone indefinitely. To be honest, I hadn't, either. But when I made the reservations, I thought it was important not to put a deadline on this period of growth in any way. This trip was about me finding myself, and who knew how long that would take?

"Sorry about that whole Tomika situation. I told Brandi it was pointless, but she seems convinced that Mika will change your mind about leaving."

I chuckled and glanced back at the striking beauty still reclined on the couch.

Jared gave me a sidelong glance with one brow raised. "Did it work?" he asked.

"I mean, she's sexy as fuck and definitely seems interesting, but..." I let the thought trail off as I shook my head.

"I didn't think so," Jared said with a laugh. But his laugh sounded strange. A bit forced. "I think Brandi is taking this a little hard, so excuse her if she goes a little overboard today."

"I expected nothing less," I said, taking a swig of my beer.

"What did you decide to do with your condo?"

"Juana's gonna move in."

He gave me another look. "You serious? You're so particular about your space. I can't believe you're gonna let lil' sis move in. You know she's gonna trash it, right?"

"Eh... I thought about that, but honestly, I'll probably end up selling it to her in the end. When I come back—"

"If you come back," Jared corrected.

"No, when I come the fuck back," I reiterated, "I don't think I'm gonna want to move back in there."

"Wow, you're really burning it all down, huh?"

"Isn't that what you suggested?"

"I said take a fucking vacation, Tomás. Not fall off the grid," he spat.

"Well, I have the kind of life that requires a real disconnect.

Believe me, if this could be resolved with a seven-day cruise, I would've done that."

"So you're clear on what you need to escape now?"

"Definitely. I was always clear on that," I said with a nod.

"Care to share?"

"Nope."

"Figured as much," he said, a smile quirking the corners of his mouth as he brought his beer to his lips. "You're good, though, right?"

"I mean, yeah. I'm fine. Just a little anxious, I guess. It's a big trip. I had to put a lot of things in motion to make sure my business continues to run smoothly in my absence. It's just a lot. I'm not used to so much...chaos."

"Chaos?" Jared questioned. "Most people would call it an adventure."

"I know. I'm trying to embrace that. Embrace the uncertainty."

"I get it. Me and mom talked about it, too. She says that you shared some things with her while we were in Charleston that may have led to this."

A scoff escaped me before I could rein it in. "Yeah, that trip to Charleston kinda highlighted the fact that my life has been on pause for a while. And when I got back, seeing you with Bran and noticing that almost everyone around me was settled and happy really drove it home for me."

"So, that's why you're going to Costa Rica? To find a wife?"

I laughed but took a moment to give that some thought. "I'm going to Costa Rica to find my fucking self, but if I find a wife in the process, that'll be a bonus."

"Well, I hope it works out for you, Tomás. I mean, I'm still pissed that you're leaving, and I'm gonna miss you, but I hope you find what you're looking for down there. It's been unnerving to have the most optimistic guy I know lose that."

"I know. Thanks, Jay," I said, giving his shoulder a squeeze.

The patio door slid open behind me, drawing everyone's attention to Tomika, who was hanging on the door jamb. "So I really hate to be that guest, but a bitch is hungry. Is that deep-fried turkey ready or nah?"

Jared rolled his eyes and lifted the lid to check the temp on the turkey. "Tell my lovely wife that we can serve dinner in thirty minutes."

Brandi had really gone all out with the decorations. The dining room was festooned with cornucopias, decorative corn, fake fall leaves, and little turkey nameplates. She'd seated me next to Tomika. The leggy young doctor flirted shamelessly throughout the whole meal. I wasn't a man who was unaccustomed to this sort of attention, but I felt weird about it since Darcy. Like I was cheating or inviting attention that would make someone think I was single, which was ridiculous. I was single. No promises were made between the two of us that night, but I still felt like I was hers.

"Ahem!" Brandi stood up after clearing her throat and tapped her fork against her wine glass. "Can I have everyone's attention? I'd like to say a few words."

I set down my fork, wiped my mouth, and gave my attention to the hostess.

"First, I want to thank all of you for coming to our first ever Friendsgiving. I'm super grateful to call of you my friends, and I hope this is the first of many holidays we get to spend together."

"Thanks for having us, and compliments to the cook! You did your thing, Bran!" Tomika said, raising her wine glass.

Everyone at the table echoed Tomika's sentiment and raised their glasses to Brandi, who smiled and got a little teary-eyed as we all took a drink.

"Also," she continued. "This Friendsgiving is a going-away party for our dearest friend, Tomás. He's heading to Costa Rica tomorrow morning, and..." she paused and bit her lip. "And I know you're Jay's best friend, but in the year or so that we've been dating, you've sorta become my best friend, too."

"Bran—"

"No, stay there. I'm fine. I promise! I just want you to know that we love you, and we will miss your meticulous ability to plan and manage every project, to always see the bright side of the worst situations, and help me keep this one in line." She hooked her thumb at Jared, who rolled his eyes. "We love you, Tomás." Brandi came around the table, and I stood so that she could give me one of her hearty hugs.

"Aw, look at you," Jared said, coming to join the two of us. "Both of y'all have always been huge saps. Just soft as marshmallows," Jared said, then pulled me into a hug that ended with both of us crying a few thug tears.

"A'ight, that's enough of that shit," I said, shoving him away to get a hold of myself.

"Agreed. And enough of this wine," Jared agreed. "Let's open that bottle of Marrow Bone Creek mom sent."

The bottle was opened. More food was served, and I polished off two slices of sweet potato pie that tasted like they were made using Minerva's recipe. The whiskey and reminiscing didn't help my mood, though. By the time we had to say our goodbyes, we were all emotional. Jared was barely holding it together. I wasn't doing a great job of it, either. Brandi was inconsolable.

"Remember to wear long sleeves and pants whenever you're outside. Dengue fever is still a thing down there. Also, make sure you send me your address when you're settled so I can send you bug repellant," she ordered between sobs.

"Bran, I'm sure they have places to buy repellant there—"

"Assume nothing, Tomás! Promise me, you'll send me your address."

"Okay, I promise," I said, giving her one last squeeze. She let me go, and I turned to face Jared.

"Make sure you call us as soon as you land," he said, pulling me into one last hug. "As a matter of fact, I expect to hear from you often. Chicago and Costa Rica are in the same time zone, so no excuses."

"You checked the time zones?" I asked with a surprised laugh.

"Of course, I did," he said as if it was normal for him to be this thoughtful, but then I had to check myself on that. Jared had grown up a lot in the last few years. He wasn't nearly as shallow and self-centered as he used to be, and he deserved credit for that.

"I'll call you when I land, and at least twice a week while I'm away," I promised, pounding him on the back. "How else am I supposed to keep you up to date on how my wife search is going?"

He laughed and pushed me away. "Get out of here before I break your legs or something to keep you in the country."

My Uber pulled up to the curb, and I stumbled down the steps, apparently a little more drunk than I realized. Opening the rear passenger door, I turned to where they stood and waved one last time. The goodbyes had gone on long enough. If I lingered much longer, I would never leave.

————

MY FIVE A.M. alarm woke me long before I was ready to get out of bed. I'd spent the rest of the night drinking with Juana, who had already moved most of her things in, while flipping through a photo album she'd dug out of the closet in my spare room. There were quite a few pictures of me and Darcy in there. I wanted to call her, but I never worked up the nerve, though. It was probably for the best. I did, however, stay up all night reminiscing about those eighteen hours we spent together, which left me groggy and grouchy for my early morning flight.

Anxious to get to sleep as quickly as possible, I found my seat in business class and began to stow my bags.

"Excuse me, Mr. Martinez?"

"Yeah?" I answered, still trying to maneuver my bag into the overhead compartment.

"It's your lucky day, sir! You've been bumped up to first class."

Frowning, I turned to look at her, one hand still holding my unsecured bag in place. "What?"

"You've been upgraded to a first-class seat! If you just grab your things, I can escort you—"

"What? Why? Is this some sort of promotional sky miles credit card thing?"

"No, sir," she said, smiling awkwardly. "You've been gifted this first-class seat by another passenger."

Okay, that was just odd. "I've never heard of this before. Is this something you do often?"

"Not often, but it does happen on occasion. Could you just grab your things and follow me?"

"Honestly, I'm fine here in business class. Can't you just go back to the customer and tell them to give it to someone else?" Because now I was envisioning an hours-long plane ride next to someone I didn't know, who wanted to chat instead of letting me sleep.

"No, Mr. Martinez. This passenger gifted the seat to you specifically."

I narrowed my eyes at the flight attendant. There was no good explanation for why this person chose me, but there was a line queueing up behind us, and it wasn't worth holding everyone up.

"Fine," I said while collecting my carry-on and laptop bags. "After you."

The flight attendant beamed as she escorted me from the very last business-class seat up to the curtain that separated it from the first-class section.

"So what happens to my seat?" I asked as she pulled back the curtain. I knew it was disrespectful to react this way to a gift, but I couldn't help feeling irritated.

"You can be refunded, or you can pay it forward by gifting it to another passenger."

"Paying it forward seems like the right thing to do."

"That's very generous of you, sir."

"And you can't tell me how I was chosen or why?" I asked, following her into the quiet spacious cabin filled with just four rows of wide, comfortable seats.

"Well," she said, stopping next to a row near the middle. "You'll just have to ask her yourself." She gestured in the direction of my seatmate. It was a woman, but I could only see the back of her head. Then she stood and turned to face me, and all the air left my lungs.

Copper brown eyes, that nose she'd given to her son, lips and a smile that I'd fallen asleep dreaming about more nights than I could count. "Darcy?" I croaked in disbelief.

"Hey, Tommy," she said with a shrug and a nervous smile. "Surprise?"

I blinked and then blinked again because this had to be a dream, right? I was already asleep back in business class, and I was dreaming about her pulling this stunt because this couldn't be real life.

"I know this is unexpected and kind of reckless. Hell, maybe you're still upset with me, and you don't want this—"

"Wait," I said, holding up my hand to stop her nervous rambling. "Want what? What is even going on?"

"I'm coming with you."

"You're coming with me?" I parroted. Did that mean what I thought it meant? My heart was pounding so loudly that I could barely hear her or make sense of my own thoughts.

Darcy took my hand, and that skin-to-skin contact made me aware of her in a way that the shock had dampened. That scent of hers — the expensive perfume that was like roses or magnolias — filled the space between our bodies.

"Tommy... I haven't been right since the day you left."

"Me, either," I mumbled, still staring at our linked hands. I was afraid to actually believe in this moment because if it wasn't real? There was no place on Earth I could escape the hurt I would feel when I woke up from this daydream.

"You know, I read somewhere that a quick, hot affair with a younger man was supposed to yield positive results. It was supposed to strip me bare, awaken new passions, new sensations, new ways of being."

"I didn't do that for you?" I asked, finally looking her in the eye.

"That's the thing, Tommy. You did. Being with you awakened me to the fact that my life was more than a little dull without you. That just having you in my home and in my bed for one night had changed the light in every room. Everything is different. Sounds don't even carry the same anymore. I felt like a ghost in my own home."

"Hermosa," I whispered, stroking a finger down her soft cheek. "I didn't know it would hurt you like that."

"Neither did I, but it was the motivation I needed to make me brave enough to make a big change in my life. I sold my brokerage, leased my house, and now I'm here with you because I'm done making myself miserable."

Stunned, I dropped my bags in the aisle and sat down. Did I hear her right? Did she just say she blew up her whole life to be with me? I stared at her in disbelief as she sat next to me. Distantly, I was aware that the whole of first class was probably eavesdropping on our conversation, but I couldn't find it in me to care. I couldn't care because I was too fucking captivated by this beautiful woman sitting across from me with eyes that caught and held the light.

"Say something, Tommy," she begged softly. "Say something, or I'm gonna think you don't want me and that I've made a huge mistake."

I frowned. "Don't be ridiculous, Darcy. Of course, I want you. Come here," I said, beckoning her to me.

A sound that was part laugh and part sob spilled out of her as she climbed into my lap and pressed her lips to mine for a shy, hesitant kiss. The first-class cabin erupted in applause — obviously, they'd been waiting for some sort of sign that Darcy had pulled this thing off. I felt the smile on her lips and heard the little kitty growl she made when I gripped her side, pulling her in tighter.

"I can't believe you did this," I muttered, closing my eyes and pressing my forehead to hers.

"Easiest decision I ever made."

"So we go to Costa Rica, and then what?"

She smiled shyly, and her cheeks flushed a dusky pink.

"We take our time. We fall in love, and then we decide how to break it to Jared. This way, if you get tired of me, he won't have to be in the middle of it."

"Tired of you? I've wanted you since I was nineteen, Darcy. I don't see that happening."

"Good," she said, her whole face flushing even darker.

"You make it sound so easy."

"I know it won't be easy, but I also know I want you to be mine. Don't you want to be mine again?"

My belly bottomed out like the plane had just taken off, but we hadn't even pulled away from the gate yet. "Of course I do," I managed to whisper.

"Good, because I'm going to Costa Rica with you either way. If I have to follow you to the edge of the earth to make you mine again, I will. I've got the money to do it."

Too many emotions stirred in me. The last thing I wanted was for her to have to choose between me and her son, but she'd already made that decision. I was afraid that I might lose her and him in the end, but goddamn, the thought of being hers again made me so desperately happy that my heart felt like it might push its way up my throat. "So you're just gonna stalk me if I say no?" I asked, trying to lighten the mood.

"To the edge of the earth," she growled playfully through clenched teeth.

"In that case, yes," I whispered, nodding my head. "Fuck, yes. I want to be yours, Darcy."

A smile dawned on her beautiful face that nearly undid me. She reached for me with frantic hands, and I met her kiss with the same urgency. I tasted her promises and delighted in the way she grabbed fistfuls of my shirt and squirmed in my lap because she could feel how hard I was for her.

"Ahem!" The flight attendant snapped our overhead compartment closed. "Please find your way to your seats! We're just finishing up some last-minute paperwork and should be underway shortly..."

We looked up at her, and the woman gave us a secret wink but gestured for Darcy to get in her own seat. And she did, but not without a moan of complaint. The moment we were buckled in, her hands were on me again, grabbing shamelessly at the bulge in my jeans and nipping at my lips.

"How long is this flight again?" she asked.

"Five and a half hours. Can you make it that long?" I asked with a grin.

"I guess I'll have to try," she said with a sigh. "It's just as well, though. You look a little tired. You should try to sleep because I plan to use you the moment we touch down."

I bit back a smile and settled into my seat. "Yes, Darcy."

Yes, always. Yes, forever. Absolutely, yes.

ACKNOWLEDGMENTS

"These times of woe afford no time to woo." I think that goes double for times of pestilence — I'm sure Shakespeare and Sir Paris would agree. Either way, it was hard to write this book because I was so homesick for a city not even four hours away and pining for human interaction that I couldn't have during a pandemic. This manifested in strange ways with Darcy and Tomás. So much longing...even when they were in the same space. Goodness. It was intense. I hope y'all enjoyed it!

While writing this, I opened a private writer's group for the #20kin5Days crew called Wordmakers. We've been breaking the place in, and I'm so lucky and happy to have them as part of my journey in this here writing life. So shout-out to my coven of writers who always make it easier to get shit done, and the group chat, now lovingly dubbed LLC Twitter, who always motivate me to push beyond my comfort zone.

Thanks so much for reading and always being excited for my stories!

WANNA KNOW WHAT HAPPENED IN COSTA RICA?

I never intended to write another word about Darcy y Tomás. I was perfectly happy daydreaming about them in falling in love in that wild country.

But you were not satisfied with that, dear reader. You wanted more.

If you want to know what happened in Costa Rica and how Jared took the news about his best friend and his mother getting it on.

Read: She Said Yes

Printed in Great Britain
by Amazon

42072700R00129